PLOWING THE PLOW

A SENTIENT OBJECT ROMANCE

OBJECTS OF DESIRE

ANNARA LAYNE

A NOTE FOR READERS

This book is, at its core, about grief: over disability, over losing parents, and over leaving home.

The main character has Ehlers-Danlos Syndrome, and there are mentions of dislocations and other EDS symptoms.

The book opens with her returning to her childhood home to clean out her parents' house a year after their sudden deaths.

I have done my best to approach these topics with care. These themes are very present alongside the levity and the smut.

Please be gentle with yourself as you read.

CHAPTER ONE

THE SUN SPARKLES over the lake in the distance, creating a bright and cheery atmosphere. The spray of orange and red leaves bowing overhead to make a canopy above the private road only adds to the effect. It looks like a postcard for the perfect autumn day.

But today is far from perfect.

Driving down the mile-long packed dirt is bittersweet. At best. Honestly, even that is pushing it.

I idle in front of the gate at the entrance to the driveway as I gather the courage to confront the task ahead of me. Growing up, all I wanted was to work alongside my parents, take over the farm once they were ready to retire, and raise my own children in the fields my family has cultivated for generations.

The thing about dreams is they change. Sometimes so slowly you don't realize you're in a nightmare until it's way too late, and there's nothing you can do to wake yourself up.

I sigh and get out of the car, unlatching the gate so I can drive through, then getting out again to close it behind me, and the whole time I'm thinking of my mom's insistence that she would one day get an automatic gate so we wouldn't have to keep getting in and out like this.

I knew she'd never do it.

And now she never can. The gate probably hasn't even been opened since I drove away a year ago with damp cheeks and stinging eyes.

An incongruously cheery song comes on the radio, something boppy I've never heard before. Some girl with an impossibly sweet voice is singing lyrics punctuated with a lot, and I mean a *lot* of "la, la, las" in between them.

A part of me recoils at the sheer bubbly happiness of the song. But another part of me is fortified by it, and I grasp onto it, building a wall of happiness around myself.

Lord knows I'm gonna need it.

The drive to the parking area feels shorter than it did in my childhood, back when the trees overhead felt like a portal to a magical land and coming home felt like an adventure. Now it just feels sad and final in a way I didn't expect to feel for at least another forty years.

The grass doesn't grow quite as tall at the end of the drive because of all the cars and trucks and occasionally tractors that park there and drive all over it. Or at least, it didn't *used to* grow as tall. After a year without the constant traffic, the grass there is every bit as tall as the lawn. It's that sight that finally makes me break down. Huge, heaving sobs wrack through me, even as I try to hold them in. I can't cry. I have too much to do.

I open my car door and step into the grass. It comes almost up to my knees, and I feel a flash of guilt. My parents and Grandpa Joe would have never let it get this tall.

But then something catches my end and I bend forward, grabbing at the little spray of green.

A four-leaf clover.

"Everyone's wrong about these things, you know," my mom used to say whenever she found one. "They say they bring luck. But it's more than that: they're a sign that big change is coming, so you better leave yourself open to the possibility. I found one of these moments before meeting your father, you know."

I cradle the clover in my palm. Change is coming, all right. But I resigned myself to the possibility long ago. I have a week to clear everything out of the house, and then the farm is going on the market, ready to be sold to the highest bidder.

Last time I was here, this part of the driveway, what my

family affectionately called the parking lot even though it's really not all that big, was absolutely crawling with people. Today it's just me, my car, and that one rusted out shell of an old Ford that's been here for ages that for some reason nobody ever took to the dump.

I guess that'll fall to me now.

My hip twinges as I grab my bags from the trunk and carry them to the porch, carefully pinching the stem of the four-leaf clover between my thumb and pointer finger so it doesn't get crushed. I might not believe in the magic of the clovers like I did when I was a little girl, but I still can't bring myself to treat it as anything less than magical.

I drop my two small bags at the top of the stairs and dig through the backpack for my keys. My mom would be horrified if she saw how little I brought for this trip—just my backpack and a carry-on-sized suitcase—but I'm not planning on staying. I need to clear out the house, get everything settled, and then sell the place that holds all my best memories.

The place that once held my entire heart.

The place that eventually shattered it beyond repair.

The porch creaks under my feet, the ancient wood finally starting to sag just the tiniest bit. I make a note to call Mr. Larry from next door to fix it, before I remember it's not my problem anymore. The porch is just one of many things the next owners are going to have to take care of—if they don't tear the whole house down.

My stomach sinks at the thought, but then my hand closes around my keys and I welcome the distraction.

My key sticks in the lock, but I finally manage to turn it, and the door swings open with a quiet creak, which shows just how bad things have gotten in the year since my parents died—they would have been horrified at the thought of the door making any noise at all. They would have grabbed the WD-40 and oiled the hinges until it opened so silently a cat couldn't hear it.

I grab my bags and head inside, kicking the door shut behind me. As much as I'd love to believe I can find a buyer who'll cherish this place as much as I do—*did*—that's simply not realistic. Oiling the hinge would probably just be a waste of my time.

A pang twinges in my chest at that. It's not like I *want* to sell the farm. But I can't keep it either, not without hiring a whole lot of labor I couldn't even begin to afford. Thinking about staying will do nothing but make me wish for an alternate reality that can't exist.

I leave my bags by the door and drag myself up the stairs to my old room. My parents were sentimental, but they were practical, too, and the only other time I came back after moving away, I didn't know what to expect: if they'd care more about preserving my room to hold onto a part of me after I moved away, or if they'd clear it out so they could use that space for something else. After all, one of the cardinal rules on a farm is to not let anything go to waste.

Last time, tears sprang to my eyes as I pushed the door open and saw my room exactly how I'd left it—and it happens again now. The room even smells the same, like my favorite lemon verbena candle. There's one sitting on my bedside table, and it's pristine, the label un-torn, and the lid is off. I always snuff out my candles by putting the lid on. After the first burn, the lid only comes off while it's lit.

I drop to the floor and sob at the realization that not only did my parents waste a whole room in their house just to make it clear this place was still my home, they also bought the exact same $30 candle I like so the space would still smell like me in my absence.

And I didn't even come back to visit.

I don't know how long I lay crumpled on the floor, sobbing over everything I've lost—my parents; Granda Joe; a body that actually does my bidding; my *home*. When I finally stop crying, I realize the clover has fallen to the floor, and I pick it up as gently as I can. It's wet with my tears, but unharmed. That's a small mercy, at least. I place it next to the candle and grab my bags from downstairs.

I have nine days to clear out the house. Gotta love living in a capitalist hellscape. Even grief isn't a good enough reason to miss more than a few days of work; and I only have a full week off because Monday and Tuesday are staff development days that I was already deemed too unimportant to have to attend.

So, I have a little over a week to fully pack up multiple generations' worth of life. No big deal.

The attic door creaks down slowly, revealing a dark hole beyond. I flip the light switch and climb the rickety ladder, wincing as my hip twinges with each step. My hips have both been relatively stable lately, but I can still feel the ball of the right joint scraping the socket when I bend it or put weight on it, and I just hope everything stays where it's supposed to be for the next week; I can't afford a dislocation, *especially* of my hip, on top of everything.

It's the perfect reminder of why I moved away in the first place. Of why the little girl whose whole world revolved around her family's farm grew into a woman who didn't step foot on the property unless she absolutely had to.

I am, quite literally, not built for this shit.

CHAPTER TWO

THE NEXT MORNING dawns bright and early. I'd almost forgotten what it's like to be on the farm, how my body will rise with the sun whether I want it to or not. I was so shocked when I moved away for college and slept through a 9 am—I'd only ever needed alarm clocks when I had to be up before dawn.

Today's goal is to walk around the farm and take stock of everything so I can build an inventory list and assess the condition of the fields and equipment. An auditor will do it again before the sale, but I don't want to leave it entirely up to someone I've never met before. Not when it's something as important as my family's legacy.

A legacy no part of me wants to let go of.

But as I slip my braces on (one on each ankle, one on each knee, and one on my right wrist), I'm reminded of the fact that I really don't have a choice in all this. My body is not the body of a farmer. My joints slip in and out, and that makes me a liability on the field. Enough so that I almost died as a teen because of it.

Other people almost died because of it.

So the farm has to go, because I refuse to let it be the literal death of me—or anyone else.

I walk a slow circuit around the house, surveying the garden, the house itself, and the chicken coop, which is filled with chickens I tried to relocate last year—but apparently, they came back, and it looks like most of them survived. Which, if you know anything about chickens, is a damn miracle.

I grab the over two dozen eggs from the boxes, making a mental note to check them all before I use any—I don't want to risk cracking a rotten egg, and there's no way of knowing when these were laid. I talk quietly to the chickens so they don't attack me for the theft, putting on my bravest *you remember me, I'm a friend, trust me you want me to take your eggs* voice. I've always been uneasy around the birds, something my dad used to fondly tease me about.

I can almost hear his voice now as I shuffle quickly back to the door of the coop, keeping one eye on the hens. *They're birds, and you're a farmer. In fact, they're your birds. What could you possibly be scared about, chickadee?*

They might have been my birds, but they looked at me with murder in their eyes. Everyone says birds are descended from dinosaurs—which I never understood, because, aren't most animals?—and I really feel like you can tell when you look at a chicken. Their beady little eyes just scream that their ancestors were ancient predators that used to rule the world.

I leave the eggs on the porch, knowing my parents would fuss at me for doing so—it's the perfect way to attract snakes, rats, foxes, and who knows what other kids of critters to the house. But frankly, if they haven't stolen the eggs out of the coop by now, they're not gonna come up on the porch in broad daylight to do so.

I make my way to the old barn, which has been a tool storage shed for most of my life. My Grandpa Joe grew up with livestock, and he always wanted to have them here on the farm he started with his brother, but he never transitioned the fields over from crops to sheep or cows. He kept some horses for a bit, to help with the work, but they only took up a fraction of the space in the barn, and by the time I was born he was already phasing them out. What few animals we did have in my lifetime—a flock of chickens, three goats, a horse, and a donkey—lived out in the old small paddock by the house

The door to the barn swings open with a creak, but unlike

with the front door of the house, this creak is comforting and familiar.

"A barn's gotta creak," Grandpa Joe would say. "Gotta know if someone's trynna make off with your livestock. Or your tools, as it were."

His thick drawl barely trickled down to me. My mom's accent was lighter than his, and my dad was a city boy from up north, so you can only tell I'm from here where I'm really tired, really mad, or around other people with strong country accents.

I step inside the barn, coughing when my foot kicks up a swirl of dust. It smells like hay and horses, despite the fact it's been decades since it's housed either of those. Fertilizer lines the left wall, small tools are arranged on the right side, and the larger tools are piled up toward the back in a shadowed clump that used to scare me when I was a child because it looked like a many-limbed monster—and was the perfect hiding place for copperheads.

I flip the switch to turn on the overhead light, and it flickers on with a low buzz, casting a hazy yellow glow over everything. It's honestly not as bad in here as I expected, and I think if I really focus, I can get through it all today. I'm not selling any of the equipment—it'll be included with the farm—but I'd like to have an idea of how much it all costs, so I'll know whether I agree with the assessor's opinion.

There's not much that's worth anything in this shed. My parents sold off a lot of equipment over the years, downsizing wherever they could. Then, once it became clear I'd never be able to take over the farm, they started pouring their money into other things.

Mostly my medical bills.

So nothing is the newest version—though newest doesn't always mean best, so we *always* had a lot of old equipment on the farm, even when my parents had the money to replace things without having to think too much about it.

Family farms don't make a lot of money, but we always had

enough for everything we needed. More than enough, truth be told. That's what happens when a city boy from a wealthy family marries into the farm.

But he's not here anymore, and neither is the money. They spent it all on ER visits, MRIs, surgeries, braces, and medications that were never guaranteed to work.

All for me.

I buckle down, relishing in the scent of those long-gone horses and hay as I take inventory of everything that's in the shed. It goes quickly at first—I can't look up the worth of everything in here on my phone, not here where the connection always drops, so I just write everything down with the brand name and serial number whenever that's easy to find.

It goes fine until I get toward the bottom of the pile of equipment heaped toward the back of the old barn. Old wheelbarrows, mowers, tillers, and more lay discarded: things that probably should have been given away or, frankly, tossed long ago.

That's when I see the plow.

My grandpa bought it when he was around my age. He used to love telling the story about how he got it at a market when he went to look for things to decorate the guest room in the newly constructed house—the room that eventually became mine. The vendor apparently had a booth full of random things, and the moment he saw this plow he knew he had to have it for the farm he and his brother were just starting to plan. She sold it to him for cheap enough that he felt bad taking it, but she insisted.

It was the best plow he ever used. Newer and supposedly better ones came along, but he was loyal to that plow until the day he died. My parents never cared much about it, but he made sure it was the first plow I ever used, and some of my best memories are of the two of us out in the field, working the ground to prepare it for whatever we were planting that year. He swore there was something special about the plow. "It's magic, Jackie Jack," he'd tell me in a whisper, like it was a secret just between the two of us. "Whatever you plant in land plowed by this very plow'll thrive. I've never had a bad harvest off this thing."

It was true, though my parents chalked it up to other things: him being such a good farmer, or luck, or coincidence (which my mom always said was a different thing than luck entirely).

Whenever I pushed the plow through the soil, it felt magic, like it was better than any other tool we could have used, like it had a connection to the land. I loved it so much that Grandpa Joe left it to me in his will.

I guess my parents didn't feel the magic, otherwise it wouldn't be tucked so far back in the shed.

The plow is the one thing I can't bring myself to add to the list. I don't have space for it in my studio apartment with a shared yard the size of a postage stamp and no shed to keep it in. But the thought of giving it away makes my heart ache so bad I have to sit down.

I feel ridiculous. Why does the thought of losing this plow hurt more than clearing out my parents' house? This is one piece of farm equipment that's probably well over a hundred years old; it shouldn't be harder to face than the house that contains the memories of the three people I loved the most.

But that's the thing about grief, isn't it? It's not always linear and it doesn't always make sense. My therapist would probably say that facing my feelings about the plow feels easier and safer than facing my feelings about my parents. It's a level of pain I can feel and survive, whereas confronting the full brunt of my grief for my parents would break me.

To which I would make a flippant joke and swiftly change the subject because frankly I'd rather not actually have to process my feelings, thank you very much.

I let myself cry for a few more minutes then carefully move the plow outside the barn, off to the side where it won't accidentally get lumped in with the other equipment. My tears are still flowing, and a part of me cringes at the thought of salt water landing on the old equipment and rusting it. Then again, there's barely any rust on it now despite the fact that it's been sitting here unused for years, so maybe it'll be okay.

In fact, it's in phenomenal condition overall. There's a crack in the wood, but that's been there for as long as I can remember, and it still works fine. Or at least it did last time I used it.

Maybe it's the fact that I'm saving it from the fate of the back of the barn, or maybe, like Grandpa Joe always said, there's magic in the plow. Whatever the reason, I feel much better the moment I get the plow outside, and for the rest of the day, I feel lighter than I have in ages.

CHAPTER THREE

I wake up at dawn again, and for a second, I feel great. I'm home. The air wafting through my open window smells like dirt and rain from the storm that started around midnight, and the first rays of light make my room dreamy.

Then I sit up, and my head screams at me. The headache gets worse when I try to stand, so I curl up under the covers and drink from the water bottle beside my bed until I've emptied it.

When I finally get up to take a shower, my face is splotchy and there are welts beneath my eyes—from my tears yesterday. One of the worst parts of my disability, Ehlers-Danlos Syndrome, is that I'm literally allergic to my own tears. An allergist might fight me on the semantics of that, but my tears give me hives and make my face tender and swollen, sometimes for days, and if that's not an allergy then I don't know what is.

I wash my face gently with just water, standing under the spray for longer than I should. By the time I get out, the heat has left me a little bit lightheaded, and I curse myself for it. I probably won't be able to do much of anything productive today—at best, I might have a couple hours of work in me before my body forces me to take a break.

I knew better than to let myself cry. Usually, I have elaborate rituals to keep the tears at bay, something my therapist always tried to convince me not to do...until the day I broke down in her office and she saw the immediate extreme reaction my body has to my tears.

It was the only time I've seen her lose her composure and be anything other than the perfect stoic therapist. She recovered quickly, but I saw the horror flash across her face at the sight of the giant welts that sprang up in my tear tracks. Normally I hate that; people often freak out in ways that make me feel like I have to reassure them—when it's *my* body that's doing these things, *me* who has to live with it so really somebody should be reassuring *me*. But the satisfaction I got from her finally understanding outweighed any discomfort I had, and it made her a better therapist because it forced her to understand that my aversion to crying wasn't psychological. I wasn't trying to avoid feeling my feelings; I was trying to avoid messing up my body for *days*.

I pat my fragrance-free face cream over my face, being careful not to use too much pressure on the sensitive skin, and walk down the stairs for breakfast.

And yep, I was right about not being able to work today. My right hip slips out of its socket as I'm walking down the stairs, and I barely catch myself on the railing in time.

This is why I live in a ground floor apartment: I can't trust my body to do stairs, and the first building I moved into had an elevator that was often out of service. Normally I could take the stairs fine, but on the days when my body acted up, I'd be stuck inside, unable to leave. I lost my job at the time because of it. Because I don't "look sick" according to most people.

As if *sick* has a specific look.

I drop to sit on the stairs as I maneuver my hip around, lining it up in the socket before jamming it back in. There's a rush of warmth and a split second of heightened pain before it all neutralizes. It'll be sore the rest of the day, and I'm just hoping I'll be able to bear a little weight on it. Just enough to be able to hobble around the living room and deal with the items in there, that's all I want.

When I finally make it to the kitchen, limping hard, I grab the old stool my parents have always kept in there and sit on it while scrambling eggs. I throw in onion powder, garlic powder, scallions I brought in from the veggie garden yesterday (thank god for things that grow without needing to be tended), and top it all with sesame seeds, a sprinkle of salt, and the hot sauce my mom makes every year.

Made every year.

I savor my breakfast, taking the time to enjoy every bite. We ate every meal together as a family, taking our time cooking together and sometimes spending hours at the table. The ghost of my parents lingers here, and if I close my eyes, I can almost imagine them in their chairs, my mom to my left and my dad to my right. It's been eight years since we lost my grandpa, but I can feel him here, too, directly across from me where he sat all throughout my childhood.

Grandpa Joe's death worsened my symptoms. While he was alive, I got every cold that went around, and I'd slip a joint a couple times a year. But after he died, I couldn't go a week without something slipping out. That's when my tears turned to poison, and my heart rate skyrocketed whenever I tried to do pretty much anything. I had to defer my freshman year of college in favor of doctor visits and medical tests and finding the right cocktail of medication that would help but never fully heal me.

My parents' deaths last year did a number on me, too. That's when I left my old job and started at my current one, which mostly just involves a lot of sitting and emails. It could be fully remote, if my boss didn't have an ego that demands a captive in-person audience every day.

If my job were remote, I could move back here.

I do my best to put that thought from my mind. I can't move back. There are too many memories here. Too much pain.

Besides, it's not like I actually have the choice. My job *isn't* remote, and in this market, it'll be hard to find one that is. And it's not like I could move back without a job. The house is paid off, sure, but there aren't jobs here. Not for someone whose body gives out at the slightest provocation, anyway. There's a reason I moved away.

If I don't get up soon I'll just spend the day wallowing, so I clear my plate and move to the living room. I plan to put everything I want to keep in one pile and leave the rest to box up later, but I can't physically make myself do it. These are my family's possessions, going back generations. I was supposed to have another thirty years before I had to do this. At least.

I drop onto the couch instead, pulling the quilt my grandma made over me. I never met her; she died a few years before I was born. But this connection to my ancestors makes me feel comfortable and safe, and I drift off to sleep wrapped in tradition and love.

I wake up an hour later with a headache that feels like someone is taking an ice pick to my skull and I groan as I sit up and the headache gets worse. Great. Orthostatic headaches always feel worse when I'm upright, and they can last anywhere from a few hours to a few days. I'm pretty much useless when I have one.

I can almost hear my dad's voice challenging me. "You're not useless," he would say. "We weren't put on this earth to be productive. You just take care of yourself, chickadee, that's enough."

But it's not, is it? Because if I don't get through this work, I'll have to hire someone else to do it. Someone who won't know which things are important to keep. I'll end up losing precious family heirlooms and things with no value to anyone else but massive sentimental value to me. If that's not useless, then I don't know what is.

My breaths come fast and shallow as I sort through the CDs —yes, actual physical *CDs*—in the corner of the room. Those are easy enough to get through, since I can stream most of the music. I set aside nine to keep and leave the rest where they are to box up later. Same goes for the DVDs, though I'm more tempted to keep those. The way streaming services are going, I'm worried I won't be able to watch half of these soon. But I don't have space for a two-story house worth of things in my studio apartment, so I mark most of them for donation and keep sorting.

By the next morning my hip is feeling better, and I hop on one of the golf carts to drive around the property.

Something feels weird. Different.

I can't place it at first. Nothing seems out of place, and yet I can't shake the feeling that I'm missing something as I drive past grassy, overgrown fields.

Or, at least, they were grassy and overgrown the last time I saw them, just two days ago.

It's when I'm looking at one of the fields with newly turned ground that it hits me: someone has been doing work on the farm, preparing the soil.

And it sure as shit hasn't been me.

CHAPTER FOUR

THERE'S no other sign that someone has been on the property. No trash, no fresh tire marks, no footprints in the soft ground.

I don't understand.

I check the fences along the border, but they're all intact. Someone could have jumped them—they're just wood, not electric, so it would be easy enough to do.

But why would someone do all that work? The whole town's gotta know that I won't be sticking around. The farm will be sold to the highest bidder, and it'll be a while before someone's ready to use this land for its intended purpose. Any work that's done now will just have to be re-done in a few months.

Sometime yesterday, every field was tended. All five of them. It's not a big farm, and whoever did this didn't do everything that needed to be done, but they did enough that it would have taken two people most of the day to get it all done—and that's if they used the fancy equipment that would have been loud enough for me to hear it. But that equipment is still safely tucked where it belongs, and there's no marks to show that heavy machinery has been through here recently.

I'm grateful to the mysterious person who did all the work, but I also can't shake the creeping unease. I have no way of knowing who did the work. There's literally no sign at all of who it might have been, not even a stray footprint as far as I can see.

I take out my phone and text my best friend, Jensen. He's on his honeymoon and due back in town in a few days. For a second I wonder if he came home early and did this for me, but he texts back *"that's so weird, there's no sign at all? Was it aliens, do you think? Real talk though, wtf? I'll help you figure it out when I'm home."*

I try to put it out of my mind as I run into town. I need to close my parents' last bank account, and it wouldn't hurt to get some more food. I've been living off the shelf-stable food and the couple things I brought from home, and I'm ready for some real, good food.

As I'm pulling out of the driveway I notice my grandpa's old plow outside the barn. I thought I put it on the other side of the structure, and I don't remember moving it, but the past few days are a bit of a blur, between the grief, the pain, and the sheer amount of stuff I've gotten done.

But I didn't hear electric equipment yesterday. That's probably what they used to plow the fields, and then they put it back in a different spot than I left it.

I shake my head. It doesn't matter what equipment they used. Someone did a kind, but unnecessary, thing for me, and I should just count my blessings and keep it pushing.

The drive to town is beautiful. I always loved taking the winding roads and seeing all the greenery—it's the kind of thing you'd think would get old after nineteen years in a place, but I *never* took this view for granted in all my time here.

Three of the farms on the way to town specialize in flowers, and you can smell them before you see them: gardenias and roses and all kinds of other blooms. I stop by the McCreery farm and slip some cash into the cashbox, then grab a bouquet from the stand at the entrance to their driveway. Leah was my mom's best friend since childhood, and I know she'd be hurt I didn't come say hi. But I can't face everyone knowing I'm just gonna leave again—and this time, there's nothing to come back for.

I park my car outside the pharmacy, and I don't make it half a block before people start stopping me to say hello.

"It's good to see you."

"Things aren't the same without an Oakley around."

"Jackie, honey, you should have told us you'd be in town, I would have brought you over a little something."

"How's life in the city? Still treating you well? Or are you finally coming back home where you belong?"

There's a reason I haven't come back. The more people say they want me to stick around, the more I want to convince myself it might be possible.

But I can't stay here. Not without a job, and not with the ghost of my parents filling up that house. I missed the last four years of their lives; I can't just come back now that they're dead. What kind of daughter would that make me?

Closing my parents' bank account goes better than expected —the perks of living in a small town—and it takes almost an hour for me to walk the five minutes back to my car, because so many people keep stopping me. I learn all about Mazey Jay's new baby; the groundhog that keeps eating Connie's zucchinis; the new statue of the town's founder that went up in the town square (which I haven't seen yet but apparently the sculptor really emphasized the man's ass in a way that has half the town clutching their pearls and the other half fanning themselves dramatically); and so much gossip I can't keep it all straight.

It's funny how I can leave a large city where I feel lonely and come to a tiny town where I probably couldn't be lonely if I tried. But that's often how it goes, isn't it? Cities are anonymous, and in places like Millford everyone is always in your business.

I'm aching with homesickness by the time I get back to the farm. What's funny is that it isn't homesickness for my studio in the city; it's homesickness for this farm, this town—for the sense of belonging I used to have here.

It's been miserable being back, but the thought of driving away in a week leaves a pit in my stomach.

Maybe I could find a way to stay. I'd have to sell the farm, but I could rent something smaller and look for a job. In a town like Millford, someone might find a use for me just to keep me around.

No.

There's nothing for rent, and there are no jobs. That's the downside of such a small town. Everyone has what they need, but there's not a whole lot left over after. All the hospitality in the world won't change that fact.

I sigh as I step out of my car. I've been through this all before. It's not like I just up and left on a whim the first time around. I thought of every angle, tried desperately to stay. It wasn't feasible then, and it isn't feasible now.

I almost don't notice that the plow has been moved again, but a bird trills from somewhere near the barn and I turn to look. I'm not used to birdsong anymore, and it feels magical again, like I'm discovering nature for the first time. Maybe, in some ways, I am.

That's when I notice it.

The plow is gone.

I hop out of the car and run over, where I see the grooves the plow has made, the slight indentations in the dirt. It was definitely here earlier, moved by whoever worked the fields for me, but it's been moved again in the past two hours.

It's not outside the barn.

It's not *inside* the barn.

It's not anywhere nearby.

And it says a lot about Millford that I assume someone returned to do more free labor for me, or that a neighbor must have come by to fix it, because there's no way someone stole it. Not here.

I've locked the house this past year just because it was going to be sitting empty for so long, but I honestly felt kind of ridiculous doing it. In all my memory, I can't think of a single time we locked the house while my parents were still alive. Even when we'd go out of town, we didn't touch the lock; we just let the neighbors know we'd be gone so they could keep an eye on things.

But the lock was always kept oiled, just in case. The memory of my dad out there with the WD-40 every six months brings a smile to my face, even as I continue the search for the missing plow. I can't really afford to spend much time looking for it, but it's one of the things with the most sentimental value for me. I can't just let it go.

We find room for the things that matter to us. That's why my mom always said, and I feel it so strongly right now.

Maybe that could mean finding room for myself on the farm, I think to myself. Every time I have the thought it strengthens, and if I don't shut it down soon, I might talk myself into trying to stay. Which would be ridiculous.

Not as ridiculous as the sight that stops me cold at the third field.

I've found the plow. It's halfway down a row, re-tilling the ground that was plowed yesterday. Which, sure, that's what plows do.

Except plows don't do that *on their own*. Not hundred-year-old plows without a computer system, at least. The latest state of the art technology that they use on massive farms? Sure. Little single-row push plows that are probably from the 1800s, though? Absolutely the fuck not.

But there it is, moving down the row like it's being pushed by a ghost. Or like it's possessed.

One of the neighbor kids must be pushing it. It's far out in the field, after all—if there's a short child behind the plow, I might not be able to see them. Especially if they're in green or brown, two colors I was never allowed to wear out in the fields.

"We don't want to lose you, chickadee," my mama would say when I came downstairs in one of the two forbidden colors. "What happens if we go out there to pick green beans and accidentally spend all our time picking you instead?" I'd giggled whenever she said it, and it wasn't until I got older that I realized she was actually worried about me getting run over by a machine, or getting lost in the fields and nobody being able to see me from a distance. If I passed out in the tall grass, hot pink, neon orange, or even white would make me visible. Green and brown would fade into the background enough that someone might not notice me until it was too late.

I stand and watch as the plow comes toward me, chuckling at myself for the moment where I thought the plow might be possessed.

My laughter stops when the plow reaches the end of the row. Because the thing is, when it's only a few feet away from me… it's clear there's nobody pushing it.

This two-hundred-year-old plow without a motor is pushing itself down the rows.

The grief is getting to me. That has to be it. I thought I'd processed my parents' death in the year since it happened, but clearly coming back to clear out the house and prepare to sell my family home is hitting harder than I realized.

I take a step toward the plow.

It takes a trundle toward me.

I open my mouth to say something, though I'm not sure what I could possibly say in this moment.

That's when I pass out.

CHAPTER FIVE

I DON'T REMEMBER WALKING BACK to the house—when I come to, I'm slumped at the bottom of the stairs; I must have made it this far before fainting again.

I drag myself up the front steps and into the living room, where I collapse on the couch.

Brain fog clouds my thoughts and every muscle in my body hurts. I figured this would happen at some point—my body shuts down if I get too stressed or stay stressed for too long. Hence the passing out. I've never hallucinated before, but it's not unsurprising that a grief-based flare would trigger it. This is all just my body handling the situation in the worst way possible.

As usual.

I somehow manage to call Dr. Watson—the number to the office isn't saved in my phone, but I called it enough times back in the landline days that I still have it memorized. Normally I wouldn't bother with a doctor after passing out, but I'm mindful that I'm alone out here, and experiencing new symptoms, and that things could go sideways quick. Hallucinations are definitely something I don't want to mess with.

Dr. Watson lets himself into the house, announcing himself loudly but calmly. He's good at that, the calmness in the face of whatever symptoms his patients are dealing with. He listens when I explain about the plow situation and nods gravely. "You know I knew nothing about Ehlers-Danlos Syndrome before you presented with it, but I've done a lot of research since then. In my professional opinion, the hallucinations are likely not attributed to it. But grief has a way of playing tricks with the mind. It doesn't surprise me that your mind filled in the blanks of your parents working the fields. And maybe it couldn't handle populating your parents into that fantasy."

I nod along. It makes sense, even though the haze of my brain fog.

"I don't think there's any more to it than grief, so there's not much you can do for it other than rest. I'm going to ask some people to come check in on you. Don't love the thought of you here alone with all this going on. Any dietary restrictions? You know nobody's gonna show up empty-handed," he adds with a chuckle.

"None." I don't tell him that there's already a couple casseroles in the fridge, as well as two dozen eggs, two pints of milk, and a basket of greens that were all left on the porch. Once people knew I was back in town, they dropped by. I just haven't actually seen any of them yet.

"You focus on getting yourself recovered, Jackie. You've got people ready to help with anything that needs doing, so don't you push yourself, you hear me? Doctor's orders."

"Thanks, Dr. Watson."

"Mac."

I hesitate. He's a grown-up. But then again, so am I. I guess at some point I've gotta start calling people by their first name. "Thanks, Mac."

He gets up to leave, then hesitates and turns back to me. "Probably not the best time to mention it, but Patty's retiring next month. I know you've got a job up in the city, but if you wanted to stick around, you could skip the interview process. I know you're a hard worker, and it shouldn't be too hard on the joints."

"I—"

"Think on it, is all I ask. I know this place is in your bones just like it's in the rest of ours. When I went away to medical school I didn't think I was gonna come back, but on my graduation day, this place called me home. I swear I heard my mama's dinner bell right at the end of the commencement speech, like she was saying *'alright, you've had your fun, time to come back now,'* and you know what? That ghostly bell was right." He laughs, but gets serious a moment later. "Don't forget I was there the day you left home. I know you didn't wanna leave, and there's ways to make it work if you'd like to come back, is all I'm saying. Patty's ready to step down and if you don't want to take over, I'll understand and wish you well. But I'd love to have you."

"Thanks."

Patty is, of course, the first person to come check on me. She and Mac must have talked, because she waltzes in through the front door not ten minutes after he leaves, announcing herself at the top of her lungs. The moment she steps foot in the living room she raises a single, overly-plucked brow at me.

"You taking over my job?" She's over the top and often comes across a bit combative, but she never means anything by it. Knowing her, she might be hoping I say yes.

"No, ma'am."

"Why not?" She scoffs. "It's a perfectly good job and you'd be great at it. Couldn't imagine a better person to fill my shoes. You say the word and the job's yours. And don't you dare try to tell me you don't want it; I saw the way your eyes lit up just now. Like a toddler in a damn candy shop. On Christmas. With the Easter Bunny there too, for some reason."

I laugh, wincing as my whole abdomen squeezes. Patty softens. "Oh, honey. I'll let you rest now. Don't judge me for the cornbread I left on the counter; you and I both know I can do better, and I'll rectify the situation soon."

"I'm sure it's great."

"Jackie." She drops her voice to a whisper. "It is from a box." She sounds so aggrieved I can't help but cackle. Patty glares at me for a second before joining in. "Don't look at me! I'm ashamed!" She flees the house, calling out a final "Love you, baby! It's good to have you back!"

And damn if she's not right about that.

Four more people come to visit over the course of the day—all quick drop-ins, just to bring me food and tell me how much they miss me.

"Mac told us your body's being a dick, which frankly is too much on top of everything else. It should stop."

I gasp at the voice and sit up as my eyes instantly fill with tears I refuse to shed.

Jensen, my best friend since kindergarten, grins at me from the doorway. "You want me to fight your body for you?" He sizes me up. "Bet I could win. At least let me give it a stern talking-to."

"Trust me, I've tried."

"Yeah, well, maybe you weren't stern enough. Remember that time you tried to get the horse to slow down by whispering at it?"

"I was shared shitless," I protest.

"You were ridiculous, is what you were. Move over, let me in."

He drops onto the couch and pulls my head onto his lap, running his fingers through my hair. Jensen's the person I kept in closest contact with after I moved. The best friend I've ever had, to this day. He and his husband just got back from their delayed honeymoon-slash first anniversary trip this morning.

"Shouldn't you be with Cole?" I close my eyes as he scratches my scalp.

"I'm sick to death of that man. There's only so much sex you can have with someone before you never want to see that person again. I need at *least* two hours away before I can stomach the sight of his perfect face again."

"Yeah, I'm sure being married to the hottest man in existence is so tough for you."

"It is." He sighs dramatically. "Thank you for understanding. Don't forget that on top of being gorgeous he's sweet and charming and rich *and* he adores me. My life sucks, Jackie."

"I know, babe. I know." I pat his arm, and we both laugh.

Jensen stays through dinnertime, at which point Cole joins us. The three of us eat in the living room and watch old movies, talking over them.

I have friends in the city, but nothing like this. There's a history here that I haven't had the chance to build there; it's hard to get close with people when you constantly have to flake on plans. Especially for reasons they don't understand, like your shoulder dislocating while doing the dishes. When shit like that happens, I can tell a lot of people don't believe me—they think I'm trying to blow them off with a flimsy excuse, and I don't have the energy to defend just how terribly my body functions, so we end up keeping things surface level.

Unlike them, Jensen's been there since the beginning, and Cole's seen enough of my issues up close and personal that he knows I'm not making shit up. Jensen teases me about how fucked my body is, and Cole has finally comfortable occasionally joins in.

If any of my friends in the city tried to do that, it would hurt like hell. But Jensen knows my limits. He knows exactly how far he can go before it changes from fun to fucked up. Cole is careful enough to never ever come close to that line, and I appreciate that he joins in from time to time. It makes me feel more normal, to have my friends being so casual about it.

By the time they leave, I'm pretty sure Mac's plan has worked: I want to find a way to stay. It'll hurt like hell to come back for good, but so does the thought of going back to a city where most of the people around me are strangers and I can't sink my toes into the dirt every day.

But coming back now feels like betraying my parents. Nothing's really different now than it was five years ago. It's not like they would have forced me to work the farm; they understood my limitations.

I didn't, though.

And even when I did, I didn't want to.

Watching them go out every day and knowing I couldn't help

them would have destroyed me. I let myself really consider staying, just for a few minutes. I'd need to hire help—or sell off the land, in which case I'd keep the house and build up walls around the farm.

Emotional walls; my parents would kill me from beyond the grave if I ruined the view out the windows.

The thought that I could stay brings tears to my eyes. I blink them away. I'm already flaring; I can't afford to cry now, too.

The tears keep threatening to spill, getting closer and closer to the surface, so I fill a mixing bowl with water, dump some ice in it, and stick my face into it. The cold shocks my system enough that the need to cry fades. I dunk my face a couple more times for good measure, then dump the water into the dieffenbachia in the living room. These things need so little water it's only looking a little worse for the wear after a year without any.

Although come to think of it, I wouldn't be surprised if Jensen was secretly watering it this whole time. I'll have to ask him.

By the time I drag myself to bed, I've locked my emotions up nice and tight, and my rational brain has taken over again. I can't stay, for all the same reasons I couldn't stay before. Coming home is a beautiful dream, but it can never be anything more.

CHAPTER SIX

I WAKE up the next morning feeling completely refreshed. It's rare for this to happen after a flare—usually it takes a few days for me to get back to my baseline. But I feel good enough to walk around the property. Assuming I *do* stay, which definitely isn't certain yet, I'll need to decide what to do with the property. My parents hired workers to help them, but I'm not sure I'll be able to afford the amount of work this place will need, especially since I won't be able to do any of the work myself like they did.

I pop in my headphones and sling my old bag over my shoulder. I don't bother to clear out any of the contents—a red flare, a notebook and pencil, a box of condoms that's probably long expired—and throw in a couple granola bars and a bottle of water. I set off, listening to an audiobook as I walk the acres of land that I grew up on, trying to imagine selling this place off. There are a few people in town who might want to take a field or two off my hands, and sometimes people will move here specifically to start up a farm. But I'm not thrilled about either option; if I'm going to keep the farm, I want to keep *all* of it.

I let myself just feel the land as I listen to my book. It's the newest romance by my favorite author, Gabriella Henriquez. I was on the waitlist at the library for three months, even though I requested it weeks before its release. They had more copies of the e-book, but sometimes even holding an e-reader can put a bit too much strain on my wrists, and craning my neck to look down at it can hurt my neck and shoulders too much. There's nothing worse than getting to a particularly good part in a book and having to set it down because my body won't cooperate; audiobooks don't have that issue for me.

This book starts with the characters meeting each other on a wild night out. Mason, the male main character, gets broken up with over text while he's picking out lingerie for his (now-ex) girlfriend. Iliana, the female main character, happens to be right next to him, picking out something for a spicy scavenger hunt run by the sex club she's a member of, when it happens. They team up for a night of tipsily running around the city to check things off her list, and then finally end up at his hotel together at dawn.

I reach the creek behind the property right as the door to the hotel room closes behind them and he drops to his knees in front of her the second the door is locked.

"Fuck, Mason, I want you so bad."

Mason grins up at me from between my legs. I can feel his breath against the most sensitive part of me, and I press my hips toward him in a silent plea for more.

"Greedy girl." He chuckles, and the sound sends molten fire through me.

"Mason," I whine. If this were anyone else, I'd be embarrassed by how needy I'm being. But I'm never going to see this man again after tonight, and that gives me the freedom to be as bold and uninhibited as I've always wanted to be.

Before I can say anything more, Mason's mouth is on me, hot and wet against the thin scrap of lace we picked out together when we met.

This is my favorite part of any smutty book, when the tension that's been building finally breaks. Sometimes the later sex scenes are better for the characters—and they're often objectively more exciting, because the characters are comfortable enough to know, and ask for, exactly what they want. But there's something about the first time, where we get that insight into the characters' minds in a way we haven't been privy to yet, and we learn this new side of them, that I just love.

What anatomy words do they use? Are their moans breathy

or lewd? Do they ask for exactly what they want or do they wait to let their partner explore first?

I'm normally the kind of person who can listen to any level of smut in public with a straight face, but I don't know what it is about Gabriella Henriquez…she gets me blushing *hard*. And she exclusively hires actual sex workers to voice the audiobooks—people who professionally record audio porn. So the sex scenes are truly next level.

I learned with her first book that I can only read them when I am alone.

In my own home.

And preferably already in bed.

For a second I think about pausing the book until I'm back in my room and can do something about the throbbing between my legs and the wetness that I know is spreading there…but then I realize I'm completely alone out here. The nearest neighbors are half a mile, a patch of dense forest, and an electric fence away. There's nobody to see me if just slip my hand into my underwear and get myself off alongside the characters.

I shouldn't do that, right?

But the more I think about it, the more I realize there's no concrete reason not to.

I've never masturbated outside before. I've had sex in fields—what person in farm country hasn't—but somehow this feels so much more vulnerable than that.

Plus, it's broad daylight. If someone saw me from half a field away, they'd know exactly what I'm doing.

Still, I'm in a secluded enough spot that nobody's going to accidentally see me—they'd have to walk through a whole field, round a bend, go through a small copse of trees, and then make it halfway through the field I'm in before they'd likely even know I'm out here.

And the flip side of them being able to see me from half a field away is that I'd be able to see them, too; I'd see them coming long before they ever actually… saw me *coming*.

As Mason pulls Iliana's panties down with his teeth, I shimmy my own pants off and then lie back in the field. The grass is high and scratchy enough that I consider going inside. Bed sheets would be much nicer against my skin than unkempt grass.

But then Mason groans against Iliana's sweet cunt (the author's words, not mine), and I know I won't make it back to my room. I need to get off.

Now.

I play with myself over my underwear, rubbing and teasing my clit through the soaked cotton. The feeling of the wet fabric against my fingers turns me on more, especially with all the descriptions of *wet* in the book.

Mason sucks Iliana's clit, then slowly pushes his tongue inside her. He fucks her with his tongue, thrusting hard and fast, and I don't even try to hold back my moan. I'm not in an apartment with thin walls and nosy neighbors; I can be as loud as I want to be.

The thought sends a bolt of heat right to my clit.

I slip a finger inside myself in time with the how I imagine Mason's tongue. In and out, slowly at first but picking up speed as the narration gets faster.

I circle my thumb with my clit while I thrust my fingers inside myself, and it feels so good I know I won't last much longer. The way Mason is drawing out Iliana's orgasm, I honestly might come before she does.

I'm panting and barely touching my clit by the time he finally rolls a condom on and slips inside her. I know the orgasm scene is going to be worth waiting for, so I've backed off so I can have my own at the same time.

He finally lets her come, literally thanking her for the privilege while his tongue is still inside of her.

I scream out, my own cunt pulsing around my fingers, and I'm wracked by the most powerful orgasm I've had in a long time.

The chapter ends with Mason standing and grabbing a condom from his wallet. I pause the book to catch my breath. The characters aren't done yet, and neither am I.

With my headphones silent, I think I hear something. It's probably just an animal or something, but just to be sure I sit up and look in the direction of the sound.

There's nobody in the field.

What there is, however, is the plow.

It trundles toward me, churning up the dirt as it goes.

With nobody behind it.

That can't be right.

Right now, I'm not mired in grief. I'm in a better mood than I've been in weeks. Months, even. So this can't be a grief-induced hallucination.

But it can't be real, either.

There are plows out there that are self-propelling, but they still need someone to be there to keep an eye on them. And this plow is over a hundred years old. It's frankly a miracle the blade is still sharp and the handle (mostly) unbroken; self-propelling is a far-away fantasy.

And yet, there it is, moving on its own.

And look. The thing is, I grew up in Appalachia, in the shadow of the mountains that watched over me my whole life. I grew up on stories of impossible things. Cryptids, strange sightings, phenomena that can't be explained.

Something is propelling this plow.

It isn't a battery. It's not a person; I can see that plain enough from here.

But the fact that the plow is working the field instead of, I don't know, going haywire or attacking me or just refusing to budge when it's pushed, means whatever force is behind it likely isn't malevolent.

I mean, it's being *helpful*. There's no evil spirit I can think of that would take its time plowing a field.

Honestly, if this were happening any other time, I'd probably get up to examine it, or run home and make Jensen and Cole come to check it out.

But I'm right in the middle of the first sex scene in a Gabriella Henriquez book—so, frankly, I have more important things on my mind. The mystery of the plow is just going to have to wait.

I close my eyes and press play on the audiobook, shivering at the sound of the male narrator's voice as it switches to Mason's point of view.

Sliding into Iliana inch by inch feels like coming home.

Her eyes widen, but I only see them for a second before slamming my own shut. She feels so good, so hot and wet and tight that if I'm not careful, I'll come within seconds. When I'm fully seated inside her, I take a deep breath, letting myself adjust to the feel of her. She feels so fucking good. There's nowhere in the world I'd rather be—and that includes the place I'm supposed to be right now. But fuck the consequences of missing that meeting; missing out on this moment with Iliana would be infinitely worse.

A squeaking sound very close to me makes me open my eyes, and I jump a little at how close the plow has gotten. It's right in front of me, practically between my legs.

Kind of like how Mason is positioned in front of Iliana. I can't help but be a little turned on at the thought.

I look up at it as I keep fingerfucking myself. From this angle, most of what I can see is the handle, which is looking...a lot more phallic than it should.

I'm tempted...

But no. I can't put that inside me. It would be unsanitary.

But now that I've had the thought, I can't stop thinking about it. I close my eyes and try to focus on the book, but instead of picturing Mason and Iliana, the image that comes to mind is of me and the plow.

That smooth handle sliding in and out of me.

Me clenching around it as I get closer and closer to the edge.

I pause the book. I'm barely listening to it at this point anyway.

I spread my legs wider, giving the plow a better view of my fingers dipping in and out of me. My pleasure builds with every pump, until I'm writhing and panting.

But I can't quite tip over the edge.

In front of me, the plow rocks back and forth slightly, almost like when a man flexes his hips in anticipation. I bite my lip, wishing there was a way I could fuck the plow. I'm desperate to feel it inside me. But even in my haze of lust, I'm still thinking clearly enough to know better than to shove a dirty piece of wood inside myself.

That's when I remember the condoms in my bag. They're old, but they've been kept in a closet all this time. The chances of them breaking are low. And I'm too turned on to care much about that infinitesimal chance.

I sit up, grab a condom from the box, and unwrap it.

Then I pause.

If this is some weird supernatural thing going on (I do snort at that *if*), maybe I should check in with the plow. I'm not really sure how to get consent from a sentient object, but if it can move on its own, there's clearly some sort of thought process or feeling behind it—or whatever is possessing it. And it should be able to give me some indication of whether it's interested in fucking me.

"Do you…" I pause.

"Is this—" I can't help the giggle that bursts from my mouth. This is hands down the weirdest experience of my life, and talking to the plow out loud makes that harder to ignore.

It's a plow! A literal, actual plow!

A plow you're trying to plow, a voice in the back of my mind says. The thought makes me laugh harder, but I'm way too horny to get distracted for long.

It takes a few minutes for me to get myself under control.

Those minutes do nothing to cool my lust. My clit throbs, my fingers are still slick with my own arousal, and my nipples are so hard they almost hurt.

By the time I've pulled myself together enough to ask my question, my voice is low and husky with need.

"Do you want to fuck me?" I feel ridiculous, but as soon as I ask the question, the plow moves closer to me and tips toward me, in a move that's clearly offering me the handle.

Okay, then. That is some clear nonverbal consent right there.

And considering I'm about to fuck a *plow*, nonverbal consent is the only kind possible.

My hands shake with anticipation as I roll the condom over the smooth wooden handle of my favorite farming implement. It's been years since I've pushed this plow through the fields, but the handle feels good in my hands, like it was made to fit into them.

Which, of course, makes me wonder how well it'll fit other places.

The handle is a softer wood than you'd expect a plow handle to be, and it's been oiled well over the course of its life. It's perfectly smooth, with no knots or dry spots, and aside from the grain, the color is almost perfectly uniform. It's girthier than my favorite dildo, but I've taken bigger.

I think.

Either way, its size excites me.

"How do we..." I trail off. It's not like the plow can respond.

Not verbally, anyway.

But just like before, the plow makes clear *exactly* what it wants from me.

It tips even further forward, until the handle trails down my body slowly. Sensually. The way a lover might trail their fingers or their tongue down your stomach, slowly building the tension until you beg for them to please finally fuck you. Honestly, the lube from the condom almost makes it feel like a tongue.

The handle slides down until it's nestled right up against my soaking wet underwear, then it nudges at me as if to say *take these off.*

I shimmy them off and toss them to the side, then shift to get the handle back to where it was before.

The plow notches itself at my entrance and I gasp at the fullness of it before it's even actually inside.

"Fuck me," I whisper. My voice comes out ragged, the command more like a plea.

Then the plow pushes forward, filling me perfectly.

I moan louder than I ever have in my life. For the first time, the sound that comes out of my is something that could be categorized as a scream.

It pauses like it's checking in with me, making sure this feels good and I still want this.

It feels *so* good. Nothing in the world could make me change my mind now. Someone could walk into this field right now and I still wouldn't want to stop, that's how good it feels.

I raise my hips. The angle pushes me further down the handle as the plow pushes forward. The result is a level of fullness I've never felt before as it bottoms out inside me. I can feel the slight flare at the base of the handle as it settles against my entrance, that light lip pressing against my clit.

It pulls back out slowly, and my inner walls clench around it as the widest part slides out of me. I gasp at the sensation, and immediately rock my hips forward, desperately wanting it back inside me—but it doesn't give in.

Instead, it caresses my thigh, spreading my own slick wetness along my skin. It teases me gently, kneading my inner thighs, lightly brushing against my clit, teasing at my entrance but not fully entering me.

My pleasure builds until I'm begging, and still, it continues to play with me. As if it knows exactly how much I love to be denied my pleasure. As if it knows that getting me this desperate before finally fucking me is how I want my partners to treat me.

I've been to a lot of kink parties in the city—I've found that people in the kink scene tend to be better communicators around sex, and they do a better job overall of treating my body with the extra level of care that it needs. Even if they don't understand my disability, they understand that when I draw a boundary, it's non-negotiable. The plow somehow gives me that same level of care, despite not having prehensile thumbs or a frontal cortex.

When it finally—*finally*—enters me again, it fucks into me slow and gentle, clearly not wanting to risk hurting me.

Which I appreciate. But also, right now I want it hard and fast.

It's teased me for long enough; now I need it to be rough and messy.

"Harder," I tell it. In this position, there's not much harm my body is likely to do to itself.

The plow keeps the thrusts slow and gentle, ignoring my demand. But I want more. *Need* more.

"Harder," I demand again, pushing my hips upward, meeting its thrusts and pushing it deeper. I moan as it hits my cervix, something I always thought sounded unpleasant when I've read it in books but fuck it feels so good, just the right kind of ache. "Just like that. Please. Fuck." My words are garbled and messy as my hips keep rocking almost on their own. "Please," I whine again.

That seems to be the key to getting the plow to believe that I really can take more. The change is slow, not the fast switch-up you often get with human partners, and the progression of the thrusts deepening and speeding up heightens my pleasure in a really delicious way.

I moan again, and the sound is lewder than any sound I've ever made before.

It honestly even turns *me* on a little bit.

More than a little bit, if I'm being honest.

"Oh fuck," I gasp. "Fuck, just like that."

Normally when I say that to a man, he immediately changes things up. A fair number of woman do, too.

But not the plow.

It fucks me the way I've always wanted to be fucked. Hard

and deep—but tenderly. The plow responds to my every gasp and moan, and it doesn't take long for my legs to tense as my orgasm builds within me.

When it finally hits, I scream out into the empty field, my voice raw as wave after wave of pleasure courses through me.

The plow stays inside me as I come down from the peak, and the last thing I'm aware of as I drift off is a dull ache of pleasure as it slides out of me and a quiet squeak as it trundles away.

CHAPTER SEVEN

A LITTLE WHILE later I sit on the porch for lunch, eating one of the many dishes that people have dropped off, watching the falling leaves swirl in the wind and trying to process what just happened. It would be weird enough if I had gotten myself off using the plow—if I'd been the one to slide that perfectly-polished handle inside of me and used it to masturbate out there in that field.

But *it* fucked *me.*

And look, there are a lot of stories out here about things behaving in ways they shouldn't. Strange lights that appear to guide lost travelers home, wolves that tend to injured children, objects moving from one room of an empty house to another. I grew up on stories of spirits and ghosts and all sorts of other-worldly shit. I've even believed some of those stories—I've had enough weird experiences that I can't help but believe in the supernatural, at least on some level. But I've never heard of a plow doing...that.

And it's not like I could ask someone. "Hey, so funny story, have you ever heard of a plow gaining sentience so it can fuck the brains out of the woman who's selling the farm it's tended for half a century? No reason! Haha just wondering!"

People would think I'm crazy. With good reason.

I'm honestly not entirely convinced I'm not.

After lunch I brush myself off and finish the walk from earlier, taking notes about the fields—their size, their condition, anything I can think of. I play a different book while I walk; the

Gabriella Henriquez book can wait until I'm in my own bed and able to listen without it making me want to fuck farm equipment.

The plow is nowhere to be seen as I walk around the property, and I'm grateful for that. As good as our little tryst was earlier, I know that if I saw it again, I'd be ready for round two, and I really need to focus.

I take a long bath after dinner, soaking my feet, which are swollen and sore. My body isn't made for this much walking, and my hips protest every time I shift in the water. The warmth feels good, leeching away the fatigue in my muscles, but it doesn't fix everything, and I fall asleep knowing that I'm going to pay for it tomorrow.

And I do.

I don't quite feel bad enough to spend the day in bed, but that's almost worse; instead, I have to push through, taxing my already sore body as I sort through my parents' belongings. By lunchtime my neck and shoulders are stiff, and my cheeks sting with the salt of my tears. I break for a hot shower, letting the water pressure work through the knots I've been accumulating throughout the day.

When I get out, I follow the smell of frying corn fritters and find Jensen at my stove.

He turns to grin at me, not apologizing for letting himself in. He doesn't need to; we've been doing that since we were kids.

"JJ!" He grins as I wrinkle my nose. It took years for me to shorten Jacqueline to Jackie. I'm definitely not ready for JJ yet—maybe not ever. "It's cute!" he protests, but I know he won't try it again now that he's seen my reaction to it.

"Why are you here?"

"We're eating, and then you're putting me to work. And if you thought you could get away with hiding the fact you have a job offer here, you better think again."

I groan and drop into a chair.

He points the metal spatula that he's using to flip the fritters at me. Little drops of hot oil hit the floor, but neither of us pay them any mind. This house has been through way worse. "Talk."

"I don't want the job," I tell him. "You know how I feel about doctors' offices. You think I wanna be in one every single day?"

"Well, sure. But I also know how you feel about this place," he says gently. "If you want to find a way to stay, you can. So what's really keeping you away?" He keeps his back to me as he says it, for which I'm grateful. Because, yeah. Leaving here broke my damn heart, and walking away now means letting go of the last tie I have to my parents. I have so many memories here: my parents and Granda Joe, learning to drive, getting ready for school dances and harvest festivals.

And the best sex I've ever had.

My mind wanders to yesterday, and even though I keep trying to redirect my thoughts, my cheeks are burning when Jensen turns back to me.

"Oh. My. God," he says. "Who is he? You know you can't go back to the city just for dick, right? That's not allowed."

"It's not dick."

Jensen's eyes widen excitedly. He was the first person I ever came out to, and it's not like I've never been with a woman before, but it's been a while since I've talked to him about one.

"It's not a person," I tell him, then immediately slam my mouth shut.

Jensen wrinkles his nose. "Okay I know you're not talking about a sex toy because you can take that anywhere you go. So spill."

I sigh. I shouldn't tell him. But if anyone will understand, it's him. Maybe.

"Okay, so… you know how there's weird, unexplainable shit that happens here."

"Jacqueline Maeve Oakley. *Please* tell me you're fucking a ghost. I will lose my everloving mind."

"What if I was? Would you think I'm crazy?"

"Depends on the ghost, I guess." He slides the fritters onto a plate and sets it in front of me, then mixes up a quick sauce. He sits next to me and dips a too-hot fritter into the sauce. "Start from the beginning and tell me everything."

I debate sticking with the ghost lie, but I know I won't be able to keep up the ruse for long if I'm telling him everything. So I take a deep breath and tell him the truth.

"It's not a ghost. Honestly, it's…weirder."

"Weirder how. It's not illegal, is it?" His playful tone and single raised eyebrow make it clear he's joking, but I still shudder at the thought.

"Oh god, no."

"Didn't think so, but I had to check. Okay, proceed." He takes a bite of his fritter and does that dragon breath thing to cool it down. I laugh at his wide-eyed, wide-mouthed grimace.

And then I tell him everything. Noticing the other day that the plow had moved, masturbating in the field, seeing the plow move toward me completely on its own…and then what came after, including the fact that it was the best sex of my life.

"So, your plow is alive." He says it like that's a normal statement to make, and I didn't realize I was holding my breath until it whooshes out of me in relief.

"Seems that way, yeah."

"Okay so this solves literally all of your problems, and if you don't move back, we're going to have a very messy friend breakup."

That seems like a leap, and I tell him so, but he shakes his head and uses the fritter in his hand to punctuate his point.

"Nuh-uh. You moved away because you can't work on a farm on account of your body being built wrong. You could probably afford to hire a person or two, which keeps you just barely below the threshold of viability for the farm. But you have a *magic goddamn plow.* You need people to plant, and tend, and harvest. But you don't need to pay anyone to prepare the fields. And honestly, if the plow can fuck you, it can probably spread some seeds." He winces. "Actual seeds. In the ground. I am not suggesting you get knocked up by farm equipment."

A laugh rips out of me. "Oh my god, Jensen, I don't think that's even possible. On a basic biology level—no, you know what, it isn't even biology; a plow doesn't *have* biology. I am not getting knocked up by farm equipment."

"Aw, but think how cute those babies would be. Your face with the plow's little blade feet. Adorable."

"No! I refuse! Imagine the birth, it would be terrible. Even the pregnancy; it would shred right through me."

Jensen grimaces. "Okay, fine, you have a point there. No cute little half-human, half-farm-equipment babies. But I'm serious about the other stuff. If you want to go back to the city then I'll support it, but I've seen the difference in you when you're there versus here. Even with the grief of this place, you're so much more…"

"Alive?" I whisper. I feel it, too. Like the land itself is nourishing me. It's why I rarely came back to visit; I've always known I belong here, it's just my body that suggests otherwise.

Jensen nods. "Just think about it, is all I'm saying. Because I think deep down, you already know what you want to do. This might make it more possible."

I've always loved how Jensen just takes things as they are. Maybe it was growing up queer in a small town—and before I came out, he was the only one out for years. A lot of people were great about it, but not everyone. He had to learn young to embrace being different, and he's always had so much compassion. Plus, like me, he grew up on stories of magic. But there's a big difference between being a guy who's into other guys, and… fucking a literal sentient plow.

So even though he's always been open-minded, I'm still very surprised when the next words out of his mouth are "I want to meet the plow."

CHAPTER EIGHT

I SHOULD HAVE SEEN the request coming.

And I do want him to meet the plow.

I just need to take some time to wrap my mind around it first. I tell him that, and he agrees, much to my relief. But then he suggests something much harder, even though it's something I've been wanting to do since the moment I got back.

Since before then, if I'm being honest.

"We should go to the cemetery."

His words hang between us, and the very house seems to hold its breath around us. I can't respond around the sudden lump in my throat, but he doesn't push me to. He just lets me feel my feelings as we finish the food he prepared. "Let's clear out the pantry, and then we'll go."

He doesn't ask if I want to; he knows the answer. *Yes*, but I'll say no if given the chance. So he doesn't give me the chance. I can't help but notice he also suggested an activity that would need to be done even if I stay. We're not packing up boxes; we're throwing out expired food. It's subtle, but not sneaky. And I love him for it.

He holds my hand as we walk to the car, where he puts on the playlist we made the night before graduation, which serenades us on the drive.

The sky threatens thunderstorms the whole way to the cemetery. Jensen stays by my side while I talk to my parents. I tell them what I've been up to in the city and ask them for guidance in my decision. I want Jensen to be right; I want to believe that I could stay here. But I'm scared. Hinging my entire plan on a bit of magic I don't understand, that could be taken away any second, is a big gamble.

We stay at my parents' grave for over an hour, and then we visit my grandpa. He was the first adult I came out to—and the first adult Jensen came out to, as well. In a town where we couldn't always be sure how people would react to our queerness, my Grandpa Joe was someone we knew we could count on. The one who actually explained sex after our parents mumbled some nonsense about the birds and the bees and our school just told us not to do it. He explained the mechanics, and the fact it was a decision we couldn't truly understand at such a young age—and then gave us condoms just in case because "if you're gonna be stupid, at least be smart about it." For each of our 21st birthdays he gave us breathalyzers right alongside the booze and made us practice until blowing into one when we drank became second nature. To this day I'll breathalyze if I'm gonna leave the place I'm drinking, even if I'm not gonna get behind the wheel.

Every time either of us comes to the cemetery we visit Grandpa Joe, and we make our way there now without even having to discuss it.

His headstone shines like it was just installed yesterday.

Craig Oakley
Grandpa Joe
1930-2021

He fought so damn hard to have Grandpa Joe be on his headstone. He started bringing it up *years* before he died, that's how much it mattered to him. "Grandpa Joe got to go to a chocolate factory! I'm going to the chocolate factory in the sky! I'll put down the extra cost, if that's what you're worried about." Never mind that his name was Craig, and it was an uphill battle to even get people to call him Grandpa Joe in the first place. The man just wanted to lay up in bed all day, pretending he was too weak to do anything until he suddenly, miraculously found the strength to go dance in the candy store.

And you know what? Good for him.

In the end, he didn't have to pay for a bit of it; the church took up a collection, even though he'd stopped attending when Grandma Josie had her first miscarriage. Grandpa Joe said he had no time for a god who wouldn't even let them meet the baby they prayed so hard for. Nobody tried to make him come back, but they took care of him all the same.

That's the thing about a small town. You show up how you can, and you're held when you need it.

I sit down next to Grandpa Joe's headstone with my legs outstretched so my knees don't pop out of their sockets. "I just asked mama and daddy for their advice, and I was coming here to ask you for yours, but I already know what you'd say."

And it's true. The moment my butt hit the ground, I could hear his voice in my mind. *"You hate the city, you hate your job, you hate your loneliness. Why are you letting hate run your life? Come home where your community can take care of you and help you find the love again."*

"Fine, yes, okay, I will take it under advisement. Could you at least be a little less sanctimonious about it from beyond the grave, old man?" I roll my eyes, then blow a kiss skyward. "You're up, Jensen. I'm not getting up on my own though so if you want privacy, you're gonna have to lift me."

Jensen shakes his head with an indulgent smile and drops to the ground beside me in that artfully graceless way that only people with functioning joints can do.

"Grandpa Joe," he says. "First of all, thank you for talking some sense into my best friend. Second, thank you for buying that plow all those years ago, because lord knows our girl needed a good fu—"

I clap my hand over his mouth and he cackles around it. When I don't move my hand, he licks it and I squirm away.

"Think about it. Grandpa Joe is the one who taught us about

sex. He's the one who bought that plow. If you don't think this was a gift from him, to show you that you'll be fine—happy, even—if you move back here, then I don't know what to tell you."

I don't believe in any sort of an afterlife, no matter how hard I've wished these past couple months and years that I did. Sure, I blew a kiss to the sky, but I don't actually believe Grandpa Joe is up there somewhere. I like the idea of it though. Maybe not of my grandpa magicking a plow to make sweet, sweet (moderately rough) love to me. But the rest of it. If there was an afterlife, it's the kind of thing Grandpa Joe would do: take my most sentimental piece of farm equipment and put enough magic in it to do what needs done around the farm.

Of course, it would accidentally lead to the plow doing what I need done inside my pants, as well. I snort at the thought, and at the phrasing. *Do what needs done* was one of Grandpa Joe's favorite lines. He'd say it to me when I didn't wanna do my homework, or when my parents didn't wanna go out in the fields in the pouring rain. Of course, he'd also say it to encourage us to take breaks or go have fun.

"I'm just saying," Jensen continues, "Grandpa Joe would want to make sure you get plowed every bit as good as those fields do." He cackles when I swat at him, and I roll my eyes even as I fail to stifle my own laughter.

"Come on. You've lost Grandpa Joe privileges. He's done talking to you." I haul Jensen to his feet and tug him back to the car.

But I can't stop thinking about it. It does seem like too big of a sign to ignore. Grandpa Joe was always doing what he could to take care of us and keep the farm running. The plow was the first piece of equipment he bought for the farm when he and his brother were just starting out. And it just so happens to come alive the first time I come back, when I'm packing everything up to sell the farm, knowing I want nothing more than to keep it?

For the first time, the thought of staying doesn't scare me.

CHAPTER NINE

THE NEXT MORNING, the plow is at the bottom of the porch steps when I go outside. I settle onto the porch swing with my blanket draped around my shoulders to fend off the morning chill and the egg sandwich I made for breakfast in my hands. I take a couple bites, then survey the trusty piece of farm equipment.

"Okay, what's your deal? We determined this is actually happening, so what? Are you haunted, like is this some ghost shit? Or is it magic, maybe a witch cursed you to turn into a plow a hundred years ago and the hex is finally wearing off. Or, heck, maybe someone did this to help me out; maybe you're a perfectly normal plow that was just enchanted to make my life on the farm easier. Not that I believe in that shit, mind you, but..." I shrug. Clearly *something* is going on, and none of the options make any more sense than any of the others, so here we are.

Here *I* am.

Talking to a goddamn plow.

Which blew my freakin' mind just a couple days ago.

Even just the thought of it makes me wet, and I shift uncomfortably on the swing as the ache between my thighs builds. There's so much I need to be doing. *No there's not*, a voice whispers in the back of my mind, that sounds suspiciously like Jensen, Dr. Watson, and Patty combined. If I do decide to stay, and I'm heavily leaning that way now, I don't have to do shit. I could kick back and relax, keep all my parents' possessions until I'm good and ready to get rid of them, and...

What?

Spread my legs for a plow?

Again?

The plow trundles forward, knocking against the base of the steps, like it can sense my agitation and wants to soothe me. Emotionally or sexually, I'm not sure. But I can't. I have too much to do.

No, you don't, that voice reminds me again. I blow out a breath. It's not like I want to leave. Or pack up my parent's belongings. I don't love my job, I kind of hate my apartment, and being here has been the first time I've actually felt happy in way longer than I'd like to admit.

And as I eye the plow, it gets harder and harder to talk myself into making the responsible choice. With every small motion of the plow in front of me, my desire coils tighter and tighter. My nipples harden, and because I didn't put on a bra this morning, the soft fabric of my shirt only makes them harder still.

Fuck it.

I finish the rest of my sandwich in a couple quick bites and set the plate aside, then stride across the porch. I can't fuck the plow here; the house is a little too out in the open. If a car came up the driveway, I'd probably hear it in enough time to get myself situated, but I'm not willing to risk it just in case.

This isn't exactly the kind of situation I could explain to most people.

"Come on, then," I murmur, rising on shaky legs. "Let's go back to the field so we know we'll be alone."

Instinct has me grabbing the handles as I reach the bottom of the steps, forgetting that I don't actually need to push it. But the handles feel good in my hands, and I swear I almost feel something like happiness radiating from the wood. The way a partner leans into your touch when you do something you like.

And then the handles noticeably stiffen.

It's subtle, but they're definitely harder in my hands than

they were a moment ago. Like dual erections responding to my touch.

"You like my hands on you? Want me to push you to the field?" I ask, feeling foolish for asking it out loud. But a moment later the plow rolls forward and back, just two quick times but it's enough to make the message clear: yes.

"Okay." I clear my throat and push gently. The plow rolls across the grassy ground without any resistance. Neither of us is adding enough pressure to actually till the ground, but it still leaves tracks in the grass. It's the kind of thing my parents wouldn't have cared about, not as long as I stayed away from the flower gardens or any seedlings trying to grow, but I'm mindful of it all the same as we leave the house and make our way to the distant, secluded field.

I never thought I'd consider the mere act of pushing a plow to be foreplay, but by the time we reach the fallow field I'm practically panting with anticipation. Every step I take just serves to remind me how wet I already am, and it's obvious the plow is similarly affected: the moment we're far enough to guarantee nobody can sneak up on us, the plow lowers itself and turns slightly, angling one of the handles between my legs.

I gasp the second it makes contact, my thighs flexing as the plow lightly strokes my clit through my pants. I whine, needing more contact, needing to feel it against my bare flesh.

I take a few hesitant steps. I can't walk quickly with the handle pressed up against me like this, but the way the plow moves against me with every step almost has my eyes rolling back in my head.

I don't even make it halfway down the field before my legs liquify with need. I'm crying out with every step, panting harder than the walk alone would make me, and I can't take it anymore.

I need the plow inside me.

Now.

The one downside of fucking a plow is that it doesn't have hands with which to remove clothing. I do love when a partner takes my clothes off. It's one of those things that can tell you a lot about sexual compatibility: who takes whose clothes off, if they do it fast or slow. It can be a sign of urgent need or done with reverence. I don't mind being the one to take my own clothes off, but I pretty much always prefer for my partner to be the one to do it.

But obviously the plow can't. Which is fine, especially because it's so good at everything it *does* do. I make quick work of my pants and underwear, baring myself to the elements. I slip the blanket from around my shoulders and lay it on the ground behind me, then settle back onto it. The plow nudges my side insistently, and it takes a second for me to realize it wants me to roll over.

I hesitate. So far, the plow has anticipated my needs perfectly, but I'm not sure it can fuck me well while I'm on my stomach— not without me getting into a position that will strain my shoulders and risk dislocating them.

But this plow has known me my entire life. It knows my limitations and why I left in the first place. This plow knows me better than anyone I've ever fucked knew me. I would trust it with my life.

So when it nudges me again, softer this time, I turn over.

I brace my arms underneath me, keeping them tight to my chest. The position keeps me stable and locks my arms in place so my shoulders won't take too much strain while I'm taking the plow.

A moment later my trust is proven to be justified when the plow nudges my legs apart and slides in between them. It tips forward until its handles rest on my back. And then, slowly, it runs them up and down, with the perfect amount of pressure.

I slide my arms out from under my, resting them at my sides like I would for any massage. I can't remember the last time I got one—a few years, maybe? I have to be careful with them, because if my muscles relax too much, my joints become unstable and risk dislocating more frequently.

The plow is gently as it kneads my stiff muscles. I always carry a lot of tension, but I didn't realize how much tenser my back has gotten since I came home. It makes sense—between the grief and the physical labor, of course all of my muscles will be tighter.

For the next hour, the plow slowly, methodically, works the knots from my muscles with all the skill of a professional. I can't remember the last time I felt this relaxed, and I'm practically putty in the plow's hands—handles?—by the time its touch turns from sweet to sensual. The pressure increases ever so slightly as it works its way back down my back, over my ass, and then finally to my inner thighs. It kneads the backs and sides of my legs, down to my knees and then to my feet, where it massages with enough pressure that it barely even tickles. Then it works its way back up, higher and higher until it reaches the apex of my thighs.

I come apart the moment it touches my clit, the wood instantly drenched in my slick juices. I cry out and bite down on the blanket as I writhe and buck against the plow. My orgasm leaves me panting and begging for more, and the plow immediately obliges, sliding into me with one hard thrust.

I bring my arms back under me to protect my shoulders. I have a feeling this is going to be a wild ride.

I scream as it enters me, my voice raw and guttural as I clench hard around the perfectly slick handle. Unlike last time, it needs no encouragement; it fucks me hard and fast, just the way I want it to, and it doesn't take long for another orgasm to build within me. But just as I'm about to come, the plow goes still.

"What's wrong?" I ask, twisting around to see if there's someone approaching the field. But there's nothing. My back twinges, a weird blend of sharp and dull, so I hurriedly turn back around so I don't risk injuring myself. As soon as I face forward, the plow moves within me again. Slowly at first, but it builds up to the perfect rhythm, hitting my g-spot with every thrust.

But once again, just as I'm getting close to orgasm, it stops moving.

I whine and writhe, trying to pull it deeper inside me, trying to entice it into fucking me again, but it doesn't move until I stop.

When it finally moves again, it's slow.

Tantalizing.

Fuck.

The plow is edging me.

And it is so. Fucking. Hot.

I've never really experimented with edging before; I never thought it would be my thing. I like getting off, and nobody has ever accused me of being into delayed gratification. I've perfected my masturbation technique so I can get in and out in a cool five minutes, which comes in handy when I wake up late for work or want to make sure I don't show up to a first date too horny. Whenever people have talked about edging, I've listened with polite disinterest.

But holy hell, it turns out they were onto something.

I have never been so keyed up in my life. It's like every time I get close to the edge without tumbling over it, my pleasure only heightens. The blanket is so soaked with my arousal that the slickness is spreading, coating my thighs and my stomach. I can *hear* it whenever the plow moves inside me.

I am more turned on than I've ever been in my whole life. Every nerve ending is alive and alight with desperate need.

We spend hours in the field with the plow taking me right to the peak and then backing off before I can quite tumble over it. Hours of me begging like I've never begged before, my desire hitting a breaking point that has me almost sobbing with need. And still, the plow teases me, coaxes me higher and closer without giving me what I need.

After the fifth or sixth time it denies me my orgasm, it starts to almost feel like I'm coming with every thrust. My every sense is heightened, and my clit has never throbbed so hard in my life.

I feel like I'm floating on air and exploding into a thousand pinpricks of light all at once, sobbing into the blanket as I writhe below the plow.

I never want this moment to end.

When it finally does, I swear the universe fractures around me. I don't know if I scream or moan or whimper or just open my mouth in silent ecstasy. I'm aware of nothing but the waves of pleasure rolling through my body, the pulsing of my inner walls around the plow's perfectly phallic handle. It fucks me hard and fast, plowing me right through my orgasm, and I'm boneless by the time the I ride out the wave.

The plow slides out of my, then rubs its slick handles up and down my back. Not a massage like earlier, but a gently, soothing motion that lulls me right to sleep, safe in the knowledge that I'm being taken care of.

And that here in this field on my family's farm, I'm exactly where I need to be.

CHAPTER TEN

"Okay," I say, striding through the front door of the only doctor's office in town. "Y'all have convinced me. Patty, you can retire now."

"Oh, thank the Lord." She jumps up with a grin and wraps her arms around me, rocking me side to side as she hugs me. "When do you want to start? Right now? Please say now." She's joking. I think. But I shake my head as emphatically as possible just in case.

I haven't given notice at my current job yet, and I tell her as much, but she waves me off as though that's nothing. "I'm flexible, you know that. And you'll have to get all your things from the city. You and Jensen take some time to get your life wrapped up and then you come back here and start at the front desk whenever you're ready."

"I'm not sure Jensen can take off work to help me move," I tell her. "But I don't have all that much stuff; I can handle it on my own."

"Oh, posh. My niece is his boss; he'll get as much time off as I say he should get. You just say the word, and he'll be good and clear for a week. Two, if you need it?" She peers at me with large, owlish eyes, and I can't help but laugh. She's greatly overestimated the amount of stuff I own. I could get it done in a long weekend by myself.

"I can do it on my own," I assume her. "Besides, he literally *just* came back from his honeymoon, I really don't think now is the time for him to be taking more time off work."

"Honey," she says, her tone going from gleeful to serious in a second. "This ain't the city. We take care of people here. I need you to take over my job, you need Jensen to help you move, Jensen need Noelle to still pay him, and Noelle needs me to tell him she's gotta. It's the circle of life. Hakuna Matata and all that."

"I'm not sure that's what that means." She's not listening, though. "Besides, you know Disney didn't actually make that phrase up, right?"

That makes her pay attention. "Really?"

"Yeah, it's Swahili. It works in the movie, but it's not from it."

"Oh. Fascinating." She says it in a way that makes me know she means it, and we spend a few minutes talking about other things that are associated with companies that didn't actually make them up, which leads to us talking about misquoted movie lines (did you know nobody ever actually says "Beam me up, Scotty" in all of the original Star Trek series?).

By the time she insists on walking me through the basics of the job, we've talked about what feels like a million different topics. I'm sure I could have been having interactions like this in the city, but I haven't. I didn't realize how much I missed it.

Patty tells me to head home a couple hours later, and I'm feeling much better by the time I leave the office. The job involves mostly sitting and filing and making phone calls—almost nothing that will strain my body. I'll start a week into the new year, and though the pay isn't quite as good as my job in the city, I won't have rent to worry about—and the neighbors are still dropping off enough food that I probably won't have to worry about groceries for at least a few weeks. Maybe months.

Patty hugs me again as I walk out the door. "I'm so glad you're coming back home where you belong," she whispers in my ear.

Me, too, Patty. Me too.

I spend the drive back to the farm thinking about logistics. I'll need to hire a couple people, figure out what to plant and when, and pack up my life in the city. There's a lot to do, but it feels less overwhelming than what I've been doing. I don't have to say goodbye to my parents' memories in such a permanent way; instead, I'll be saying goodbye to an apartment that never felt like home in a city where I never truly felt like I belonged.

When I pull up to the parking area at the end of the driveway, I see the plow trundling through the fields. I stop to watch it for a few minutes, feeling a swell of pride, happiness, and, yes, horniness inside me.

It's silly, but seeing it working the fields for me, without me even having to ask, feels like confirmation that this is where I belong. Like it's yet another part of my community coming together to help take care of me. Or a loving partner making sure we have an equitable division of labor.

I give it a little wave before heading inside and grabbing my laptop so I can draft an email to my boss, giving two weeks' notice. There's a little spark of guilt when I press send, because I always hate letting people down. There's nothing particularly special about my job, or my role there; I'm replaceable, and they'll be able to fill the position easily enough. But my parents drilled a strong work ethic into me, and I can't help but feel like I should stick it out until they no longer need me.

Ten minutes later I get a response saying that I don't need to give them two weeks; they're accepting my resignation effective immediately and I can pick up my final paycheck at my convenience.

It's the outcome I secretly hoped for, but I still feel a flare of panic at the realization that I have quit my job and won't be starting at my next one for a few weeks. I'm officially unemployed, something I've spent my whole adult life trying to avoid. It's probably for the best—this gives me time to settle back into the house and my life here before I add a new job into the mix.

I look around the house.

My house.

The house I've always wanted to grow old in. The house I pictured raising my own kids in, if I ever have any, and throwing holiday parties at. The house I can still feel my parents' and Grandpa Joe's presence in, in the most comforting way.

Tears spring to my eyes, and for once, I don't try to hold them back.

It feels nice to cry out of relief; I can't remember the last time I did that. And since I have the next few weeks off, I don't spend the whole time worrying about how hard the crying will impact me. I just let the tears flow, then eat comfort food in front of the TV. I drag myself up to bed once I start drifting off, and sleep more deeply than I have in a long, long time.

It's almost noon when I finally wake up, and I feel bad enough that when Jensen offers to bring me dinner and hang out for a bit I say no. Today's a couch day, a do nothing day, an "I'm not even sure I'm actually human" day, and it's the first time in a long while that I've been able to take one of those without worrying about all the ways it'll set me back. I eat leftovers and crackers and cheese and stay horizontal for 99% of the day.

When I look out the window that evening, watching the sun set over the fields as I go to bed early, I see movement in one of the fields. It's the plow, diligently working even when I can't.

That night I have dreams about the plow, well, plowing. Fields, as it was intended to do.

Me, as it recently (thankfully) decided to do.

There's even one in which I switch things up and I plow the plow instead of it plowing me—though when I wake up, the exact details of that dream elude me. Which is a shame, because I'm really curious about those logistics.

The first thing I do after waking up is head out to the field. If I had a human partner, I'd be in the mood for some lazy morning sex. My partner being a plow doesn't mean I can't have that; it just means I need to get a little creative.

And that's exactly what we do, tucked behind the old barn.

I run my hands along the metal parts of the plow, being careful not to cut myself on the blade. The condition of the plow astonishes me—after years of being in storage in an old barn that's not in the best shape, I'd expect there to be a fair amount of rust. But there's not a single speck; it shines like it's brand-new.

The plow shivers as I trail my fingers along it, and I delight in the feeling that I'm giving it pleasure, even if it's not as intense as the pleasure it gave me.

An idea takes hold of me.

But before I proceed, I need to wash it down. You don't spend your whole adolescence on a farm without knowing having tetanus safety instilled in you. The plow looks clean enough, but you never know when contaminated dirt might be clinging to something. And for what I have in mind, a condom won't cut it.

"Come with me," I coax, leading it over to the hose. I grab a bottle of soap and turn on the water to spray it down. The moment my soapy hands touch the plow, I realize my error. I thought this was prep work for the sex I wanted to have. But turns out, washing the plow is the most erotic foreplay I've ever experienced.

My slick hands slide down strong metal and the plow shudders in my hands.

I grin. "You like that?"

I grip it tighter, twisting my hand as I lather the frame, slowly pumping my hand up and down the smooth wood and metal. I'm thorough, making sure I cover every last inch in soap, and delighting in every resulting shudder the plow gives me. I drag it out as long as I can, and even though very little water gets on me, I'm soaked by the time I'm done—because cleaning has never felt so dirty.

I dry the plow with as much care as I washed it—I don't want it rusting now. Then I roll a condom onto the handle and slowly bend forward, bringing my lips to the wooden handle.

The plow goes perfectly still in front of me. Up until now, I've been on the receiving end of all of the sex: it fucked me, it gave me a sensual massage. I washed it, sure, but that could have just been good tool care. But now with my mouth on it, there's no question.

I swirl my tongue around the tip of the handle. I shouldn't be surprised that it feels different than a dick, but somehow, I am. It's firmer in my mouth, and cooler to the touch. When I suck it into my mouth, it fills the space more fully.

There's none of the usual pulsing when I do something my partner particularly likes. All human anatomy has those little tells, the subtle changes in blood flow. But even without that, it's clear the plow is enjoying this.

So am I.

I suck the handle in deep, running my tongue along the bottom of it.

Then I slowly slide it out of my mouth and switch to the other one, putting a second condom against my teeth and rolling it on with my tongue.

I can immediately tell this isn't the handle that's fucked me before. I'm not sure how I know, but it feels different, somehow. Like there's a slight difference in the shape, almost imperceptible, but I'm intimately acquainted with the other handle, enough to feel the difference.

I move back and forth between the handles, licking and sucking, and when I can't take it anymore, I don't stop; I just drop a hand between my legs. I've never enjoyed giving a blowjob this much, and I'm not about to stop just so I can get off.

And that's exactly what I do, coming on my hand while the other is wrapped around one of the plow's handles, with the other handle in my mouth muffling my screams.

Right there at the side of the house where anyone could see if they drove up.

They don't, of course. But the idea that they could thrills me in a way I never expected.

CHAPTER ELEVEN

A WEEK LATER, Jensen, Cole, and I are in the city clearing out my apartment. We pack up the few things I decide to bring to the farm, but I'm surprised by how little of my stuff I care enough about to keep.

Because the house is fully furnished, I knew I'd leave my furniture behind, but I thought I'd at least have some emotional attachment to the things I've lived with for the past few years. But nope; Jensen, Cole, and I haul most of it to the curb, with a sign saying that it's free and from a house with no pets or bed bugs (if you know, you know). By the time we load the last of my clothes and the few decorations I care enough to bring with me into the truck, most of the furniture is already gone.

Honestly the hardest part of the process was breaking my lease; it felt silly to pay for the privilege of no longer living somewhere.

There's a slight twinge in my chest as we drive away, but it fades with every minute. By the time Cole merges onto the highway, the little bit of sadness has faded completely.

I thought we'd all have to crowd onto the bench seat that spans the front of the truck, with a third seatbelt in between the driver's and passenger's seats, but I have so little stuff that it all fits into the bed of the truck with ample space left over, so I have the whole back seat to myself. It's one of those half ones, with sideways jump seats that face each other, but the truck is wide enough that I can stretch out my legs and prop them onto the opposite seat.

"Crazy idea," Cole says when we're a couple hours into the drive back home. We left bright and early so we could do it all in a day. I try not to think about how sad it is that it was possible to pack up and throw away my entire life from the past few years in just a few hours. "What if we hit that market on the way home. You know, the one we always pass and say we've going to check out someday?"

"With all this stuff in the bed of the truck? I'm not sure that's safe, pumpkin," Jensen says. He started calling Cole pumpkin as a joke one year around Halloween, pretending to be sickeningly sweet, and did it so much that it eventually became unironic. It's been years, and he shows no sign of stopping.

"Ah damn, you're right."

"Fuck it," I chime in from the backseat. "It's my stuff, and it's not like someone's going to steal it. And if they do…well, that would suck, but we've been saying we should since high school, and we've never actually done it. We should go."

"But your stuff…" Cole says hesitantly.

I shrug, even though he and Jensen can't see me. "We're going to a market. If my clothes get stolen, I'll just buy more." I sound much more cavalier than I feel, but I'm in the mood for an adventure. Besides, even if everything in the truck bed gets stolen, all the things I care about most are safely back at the farm.

Cole whoops and takes the exit a couple miles later. We expect it to be right off the highway, with how prominent the signage is, but it's almost four miles down a pretty empty, winding road. My anticipation climbs. This is either gonna be the kind of market you tell stories about for years, or it'll be…a funny anecdote, at least.

The moment we arrive, I know it'll be the former.

The parking lot is as big as the main lot for the state fair (which makes it at least five times the size of the parking lot for the county fair), and though it's less than half full, we can see a decent amount of people, even from here. After all the effort of moving my body aches, so I pop my disability pass in the window and tell Cole to pull into one of the accessible spots by the front.

"I don't have a lot of walking in me," I tell them as we look for a directory, or maps, or anything to tell us where we should go, "but there's a food court over here, so when I need to be done, I can sit and eat and y'all can keep shopping."

"You know damn well and good we're not going to abandon you," Jensen argues, but he softens at the look in my eye. "Fine. If this place is really, really good, we'll keep shopping while you eat. But we'll take pictures. Or FaceTime you. If you want."

"Deal."

One of the hardest things about my disability is knowing that if I'm out with people, they sometimes have to cut their enjoyment short for me. I love that Jensen and Cole know I'm a grown ass woman who's fully capable of keeping myself entertained for an hour or two, thank you very much. I have a fully charged phone, a backup battery, headphones, and a kindle. I'll be good.

"Okay but why isn't there a directory?" Jensen asks the question that's on my mind. We can see the food court, and a few booths along the winding path, but there's nothing to help us decide where to go.

We set off, deciding to just wander a bit—but then Cole notices an information desk.

"Excuse me? We're looking for a directory."

"Oh, we don't have one," the woman behind the desk says cheerfully. "But don't worry, you'll find what you need; people always do."

Okay so this place might be a bit of a funny anecdote, as well.

"Jacks," Jensen says quietly. "There's wheelchairs. Want one?"

I used to feel so bad even *thinking* about using mobility aids, like I wasn't disabled enough to truly need them. Then one day Grandpa Joe told me if I couldn't do what I wanted, or if I had to stop early, and the wheelchair (or a cane, or a rollator) would enable me to do it, then that meant I was disabled enough and I should use one. In hindsight, that seems obvious, but I needed to hear it in order to really believe it.

Jensen pushes me while we browse, and this place is everything we all hoped it would be. There are dozens, maybe hundreds of vendors, and they sell everything you could possibly imagine: jewelry, jams, clothes, cloth, furniture. There are fewer electronics, but there are a few booths here and there, mostly with vintage items, like those clear colorful landline phones I remember from my childhood.

Something keeps snagging at the back of my mind, and it isn't until about an hour in that I realize what it is.

"Holy shit. I think Grandpa Joe brought me here when I was little."

"Really?"

"Yeah. I didn't realize. I was really young, maybe two or three? I rode his shoulders part of the time, so I must have been pretty small. But that tree looks familiar." It's a wide oak with a wooden bench ringed around it. The bench is painted in rainbow colors, and there are strings of beads hanging from a few of the branches way up high. They catch the light, throwing little rainbows on the ground. "Yeah, he bought us ice cream, and we sat right there eating it. We talked about all the colors, and he said that finding me at the end of the rainbow was even better than finding a pot of gold. Damn."

My eyes well with tears at this surprise moment of nostalgia. But then I remember something else about that day, and I gasp at the memory.

"Holy shit," I say it a bit too loud, and a mother with two young kids glares at me as she hurries them away. Oops. "This is where Grandpa Joe bought the plow. He took me to visit the vendor who sold it to him. He told her I was going to inherit the plow someday, and told her how proud he was that the farm was going to stay in the family. That was the first moment I remember thinking that nothing could ever make me leave.

Fuck." My cheeks are wet by this point, and I raise my shirt to wipe the tears away.

"What are the chances the vendor is still here?" Jensen asks. "Do you want to try to find her?"

I try to think. In my little-kid mind she was old, but not nearly as old as Grandpa Joe—who was probably only around 50 at the time. Accounting for the fact I was too young to gauge ages, and that damn near everyone seemed old to me, my guess is that the vendor was probably in her twenties or thirties. "She'd probably be middle-aged now. So, it's possible, but I don't know if she'll still be selling at the same market over twenty years later. But maybe," I whisper. It almost hurts to hope, but I do want to find this one more connection to my grandpa if I can.

"And hey, maybe she'll know what's going on with the plow," Jensen and I say at the exact same time.

"It's so freaky when you two that," Cole complains. "You don't even have the excuse of being twins. You're not even *related*. It's creepy." He's so focused on that he doesn't ask what's up with the plow, for which I'm grateful. That's not exactly the kind of thing I want to talk about in public, especially after getting dirty looks for just saying the word *shit*.

Jensen and I grin and high five each other, then we set off to find a vendor who might not even exist anymore.

We find her ten minutes later.

I was worried I wouldn't recognize her, and I assumed her stall would have changed in the past two decades. But the moment I see the tent with strings of letter tiles hanging across the entrance, I know it's her.

"Stop! This is it!" I'm so excited I tumble out of the wheelchair before Jensen stops pushing it, and almost trip in my hurry to meet the woman. *It might not be the same woman,* I tell myself. *It could be her sister, or her son. Or she could have sold her setup to someone else entirely.* I'm trying not to get my hopes up.

It's not working.

My heart races as I step into the booth, holding my breath in anticipation.

The woman inside looks exactly how I remember her, not a day older. I didn't think I'd recognize her; I couldn't remember anything about her—not her race, her hair color, or anything else aside from the fact that she was an adult and younger than Grandpa Joe. But looking at her now, I remember her in vivid detail.

Well. Not her. Because when I say she looks exactly the same, I mean she looks *exactly* the same. There's no sign of the passage of time. My memory of this woman could have been from an hour ago for how similar she looks.

This must be the original vendor's daughter, then. It's uncanny how much she looks like her mom.

"Hi, I'm so sorry to bother you," I say breathlessly. "My grandpa bought an old plow from you—or, I guess, probably from your mom—a long time ago. I wanted to talk to the vendor who sold it to him, but I guess you probably wouldn't know anything about it."

I swallow down my disappointment. It was always a long shot.

The vendor surprises me by smiling. "I know that plow."

I know that plow.

That's a weird way to phrase that, right?

I remember the plow, or *I'm familiar with the plow,* or *I know which plow you're talking about* would all make more sense. But *knowing* the plow? Does that mean what I think it means?

"You *know* it?" I stress the word, and she smiles at the emphasis.

She knows. She totally knows.

"Sorry, I'm Jackie." I stick out a hand, and she shakes it firmly.

"Jackie. Welcome, dearest. Yes, I remember your grandfather. He used to visit me regularly. I am pleased to hear the plow has served him well."

"Not as well as it's serving her," Jensen says salaciously, elbowing me in the side. Honestly, until this moment, I forgot he was here.

"Oh?" The woman raises a perfectly shaped black brow. She gives me a knowing look.

From Jensen's other side, Cole asks "Why'd you say it so weird?"

"I…well…" I stammer. It was hard enough telling Jensen. Telling a complete stranger feels impossible.

Thankfully, the vendor, who didn't introduce herself back, swoops in to save me. "My items are very special. I operate differently than the other vendors here. In fact, I see myself as less of a vendor and more of a…matchmaker. I will not let my objects pass into just anyone's possessions. Your grandfather was a good man—the first person I placed one of my objects with, in fact."

"You look exactly how I remember you," I blurt out, wincing at the abrupt change in topic.

The vendor smiles. "The years have been kind to me. Though it's a privilege to age, and I look forward to the days my face shows the culmination of my years." She smiles, but there's a tightness around her eyes.

I don't know how to respond to that. Mostly because she's speaking like the mysterious soothsayer in a fantasy book.

"What brings you to my booth?"

"This might sound silly, but have you ever heard of any of the things you sell having magic? Like, being…possessed?"

Her eyes flick to Jensen and Cole, who take the cue to leave us alone to talk. They leave the wheelchair right outside the tent and tell me they'll be browsing nearby.

"Tell me what has happened," she says quietly once it's just the two of us. I give her the condensed version, which includes the plow magically plowing the land, but does not include the plow magically plowing…me.

"Your grandfather never mentioned this."

"I'm not sure he knew?" I certainly never saw the plow move on its own until recently, and it was the plow I learned to till the soil with. This plow was an active part of my childhood, all the way through my teen years, and it never once moved on its own then. At least, not that I was aware of. "It seems to be a recent development."

"Hmm. This fascinates me." Normally I'd hear those words and assume the speaker was being facetious, but her voice is so full of wonder I can't help but take her statement at face value.

What fascinates *me* is the way this woman speaks. Old-timey and a little mystical, but then sometimes she sounds a bit more modern.

"My objects have personalities," she tells me with a frankness that startles me. "I allow them to choose who they would like to go home with. It seems the plow chose somebody who cared enough about it to pass it to a loved one who also cared deeply for it. And only then did it show itself to you, correct?"

"I mean, we've been able to see it this whole time. But the whole sentient thing? Yeah, that's newer."

She smiles like a mother proudly talking about her child. "The plow was the first object I placed. I've spent years wondering. I assumed your grandfather simply failed to mention it's liveliness but now I wonder if perhaps he never encountered it."

"Have any of the others been...alive, like this?" She said they have personalities, but people say that about all sorts of things that aren't sentient, like cars, or colorful plates.

"One other that I know of," she confirms. "Interestingly, the sheets also chose to show themselves to a person other than the one I placed them with."

Did the sheets also fuck that person senseless? I want to ask. But I haven't even told the woman about that. And the answer has to be no, right?

Thankfully, she answers my question without me having to ask. "The sheets were always more on the affectionate side, and the young woman they revealed themselves to said they seemed to inspire amorous feelings within her. It stands to reason that the sheets would work in the bedroom and the plow would work the land."

The land isn't the only thing the plow is working.

She narrows her eyes at me as my cheeks flush, but thankfully she doesn't push the issue. Still, I can't help but wonder if she suspects what it is I'm not telling her.

We wrap up the conversation, and I promise to come back to visit so we can share stories about Grandpa Joe—and so I can keep her updated on the plow.

I find Jensen and Cole in a nearby booth. Cole eyes me curiously, and I promise to tell him everything on the drive home. That's one thing I appreciate about Jensen: as much as he loves both his husband and gossip, he won't share something this big without my express permission.

We have a quick lunch at the food court before heading back to the car. An elderly man glares at us as we get into the car, and Jensen stiffens, but I'm used to this happening. We left the wheelchair back at the information desk, and you wouldn't know I'm disabled just by looking at me.

Which is why the old man should mind his own damn business, but I'm not going to waste any energy thinking about him.

On the drive home, I tell Cole everything. Unlike with the vendor, everything very much includes the sex. He and Jensen get every little detail, and it feels weirdly normal to be telling them about it. Cole is more weirded out than Jensen was, but by the time we arrive back at the farm, he's moved past the weirdness and is just asking the same kind of overly invasive question anyone would ask their husband's best friend, who's one of their best friends as well, about her sex life.

Jensen and Cole unload my things, dumping the boxes of my clothes on the floor of my closet and leaving everything else in the sunroom.

"Can we meet the plow?" Jensen asks.

I shake my head. "Not today, I know need an Epsom salt bath. But soon," I promise.

"We're gonna hold you to that," Cole warns.

"I'd expect nothing less."

"Good. Because I can't properly judge without meeting it. My seal of approval is currently conditional." Jensen pulls me into a hug. "Get some rest. Heal fast, because I've waited long enough to meet this best lay of your life."

I'm equal parts nervous and excited for them to meet.

If the plow were human, I'd probably have introduced them by now, so it stands to reason that I should let my best friend and his wonderful husband meet the piece of equipment that's dicking me down.

Handling me down?

Plowing me.

I laugh. "Yeah. Soon."

CHAPTER TWELVE

THE PLOW DOESN'T SHOW any sign of sentience when I take Jensen and Cole to meet it.

"Cole, can you give us a minute?" Jensen asks. His husband presses a quick kiss to his cheek and walks halfway across the field, leaving me, Jensen, and the plow. "Alright, plow, it's just us three now. Me and Jackie grew up together. You know me, I spent half my time here in high school. And you know all I want in this world is the best for her. If you don't wanna show yourself to me that's fine, but I promise I'm safe. And I'd really like to meet you."

He sounds ridiculous.

And I am so, so grateful to him for doing it anyway.

"It's true," I say, not above begging if it comes to that. I came out here this morning to warn the plow that I was gonna bring Jensen and Cole to meet it, but it's not like I could understand what it meant when it nudged me in response. I took that as a yes but maybe it was saying no. Maybe it won't show itself to Jensen. Maybe it's upset I brought him to meet it.

God, I hope not.

"Jensen is the person I trust most in the world," I continue. "I trust him as much as Grandpa Joe." At that, the plow stirs, and I can see Jensen beside me trying his very best not to react. He won't wanna scare the plow away. "Thank you," I tell it, reaching out a hand. The plow rocks forward, bumping against me, and I grin.

"See? I told you it's alive," I tell Jensen triumphantly.

"I believed you. It's just so wild to actually witness it, you know?" He sounds dazed, which I get. It's a whole lot to take in. "Can I call Cole back over here?"

Rather than react in a way that we could possibly misinterpret, the plow takes off, trundling through the field. Cole watches it approach with us a good few paces behind it, and his eyes are wide when we all reach him.

"Holy fucking shit."

"Yeah, that's about right," Jensen says weakly.

"It's really…" Cole trails off.

"Alive? And fucking me." I laugh. "Wild, right?"

"I still can't believe it. I mean, I can; I'm looking at it with my own two eyes. But wow." Cole sounds dazed. Beside him, Jensen looks a little awestruck, too.

"And to think, all this started because you were listening to an audiobook on your walk. A spicy audiobook," Jensen says.

"Obviously a spicy one. I didn't exactly go from listening to a gory slasher to getting my back blown out by a plow, now did I?"

"You mean…getting *plowed* by a plow." Cole giggles, a high, almost wild sound. He's promised his discretion, but he's freaking out enough that I feel the need to remind him how important it is that nobody else can ever know.

"Cole, you can't tell anyone about this."

He sobers in an instant. "Of course not. I'm a little freaked out, not gonna lie, but I would never tell anyone. They wouldn't believe me anyway. Plus, this plow being alive is the reason we get to have you close. Jensen wants his best friend close by, and I want to get to spend more than just a few days at a time with you. Telling people would backfire on me in a whole lotta ways. I promise you I will never tell anyone."

I didn't realize how worried I was until I hear him promise he won't tell anyway—and the thing about Cole is that he always honors his promises. No matter what.

"Tell us again how it happened," Jensen prompts. "Normally

I'd make the partner tell, but, well…" He gestured to the plow, and I laugh.

I take a deep breath. "Fine. So, I was listening to my book, and things got spicy, and I figured, you know, I was alone in the fields with nobody around, and I had a blanket so it's not like I was lying directly in the dirt. And the house was so far away but the book was making me feel…certain things. So I decided to, you know, take care of things…" I'm not normally shy talking about sex, especially not with Jensen. But this feels different. I'm about to tell him about how I fucked a literal plow, for god's sake. And with the plow right here beside me, it somehow feels more awkward than the first time. "Anyway, then the plow came toward me through the field, and, well, things just kind of went from there."

I'm rushing through the story, but the plow nudges me. Like it wants me to slow down. I shake out my tension. It's right. I wouldn't be embarrassed if this story were about a person, and frankly the plow has already done more for me—both sexually and otherwise—than any human partner I've ever had.

There's nothing shameful about this.

"You didn't stop to wonder what was happening?" Jensen asks in disbelief.

"I mean, I did, but I was…I was too horny to really think things through, okay?" I yell, covering my face with my hands. But it's in a playful way, not an embarrassed one. "I just really needed to get off and let me tell you the plow got the job done, and it did it *well*."

"Well that's something, as least," Jensen says, laughing. Beside me, the plow moves ever so slightly, the handling brushing up against me in slow, methodic movements. It's caressing my thigh, I realize, trying to calm me down. Which is…honestly really sweet.

That, or it's trying to turn me on.

Either way, it's working.

"Okay, so what now?" Jensen asks.

"Now we get to work on planning how I'll keep the farm running, especially since it's not exactly like I can tell all the farmhands about my magical living plow."

Cole runs to the house for a few outside blankets and brings them back with a little picnic, and the three of us sit right out there under the cloudy sky and get to work making plans. We brainstorm the people who are less likely to question things, like why I do all the plowing on my own at night (which is the cover story we come up with), and think about when to start. We've missed the current round of sowing, so we decide we'll wait until the spring and plant then. I'm a bit relieved. That gives me time to settle back into the house and get used to my new day job before I have to add the bulk of the farm stuff to my plate. I'm a little worried about the money, because it takes a while for a farm to start turning a profit after a year of empty fields, but Jensen reminds me that the town will rally around me to help me get back on my feet if I need them to.

"Everyone loved your parents and they all love you. Nobody wants to see the farm go under. That's part of the beauty of this place: people will help whenever and however they can."

He's right.

By the time Jensen and Cole leave I'm feeling good about everything—and the shock seems to have worn off for both of them. I think watching the plow stay by my side and be mostly normal—plus, you know, the occasional sweet touch—helped.

I wave the guys off and watch them leave, and once I see the dust rise from their car in the distance, I lie back on the blanket and spread my legs. My dress tents across my knees, but before the plow can move to slide underneath it, I reach out and grab the handle, pumping my fist up and down it slowly like I did the other day. The plow stills, pushing into my hand ever so slightly but otherwise just letting me work it, and my other hand drops between my legs while I play with the plow.

I circle my clit, feeling the front of my panties grow wetter and wetter as I bring myself and the plow closer to pleasure.

For the first time, I wish the plow could come. I want to see the evidence of its arousal. I want to feel the wet heat of its orgasm splash across my skin, or feel its smooth wood pulsing inside me, filling me to the brim. Even just imagining it heightens my pleasure, and I rub harder and faster, my clit aching with a desperate need. The plow thrusts into my hand in a needy move, pushing itself harder and faster into my hand, and I grip it tight as my orgasm sweeps through me, leaving delicious tingles wracking through me.

"Fuck," I moan.

The plow goes limp, falling forward instead of holding itself upright, and it crashes to the ground beside me.

I turn toward it, the way I might look at a lover in bed. The sun catches the metal blades, and they glint almost wickedly in the light. I don't touch them; I'm boneless, too exhausted to ensure I don't accidentally hurt myself on the sharp metal, but the sight stirs something within me, and I once again think about how ridiculous it is. I've been having great sex with a plow and now I think I'm…falling for it?

But that's ridiculous. It's one thing to fuck a plow; it's another thing entirely to think I might be in love with one.

Then again, the vendor did say the objects each have a personality of their own. Me developing feelings for the plow isn't any weirder than the plow being alive, is it?

I try to think about what else she said, but I have a hard time focusing on the details of the conversation—and when I try to picture her face, I can't.

I frown. I'm great with faces—I never forget one, literally ever. My parents always called it my superpower. But hers is almost hazy in my memory, and aside from what she said about the plow and about Grandpa Joe, I don't remember much about out interaction.

The realization creates a lazy current of anxiety through me—

there, and concerning, but I'm too satiated from my orgasm to pay it much attention. It's been a long few days; of course I'm not clearly remembering the details of a stranger I met on a busy day. Sure, this is the first time it's ever happened, but it was bound to happen at some point, right?

CHAPTER THIRTEEN

By the time I start work at the clinic, we've got seeds ordered and the lots planned out, and the neighbors have even looked over the plans and given their opinions. It's the kind of thing I never would have asked for in the city—and I didn't have to here; people offered, and I couldn't have turned it down if I'd wanted to. And I really, really didn't want to.

People stop by just to say hi, and I convince a few of them to get much-needed check-ups. Something you learn quick in farm country is that farmers don't go to the doctor unless they're dying—and even then, it's usually their wives who makes them come in. The women are better about it than the men, but if a farmer comes in you drop everything. So, I warn Dr. Watson to expect a bunch of farmers coming by in the next few weeks so he doesn't think the entire community is dropping dead all at once.

The first week in the office passes quickly, as does the second week. Before I know it, a whole month has passed, and Patty is officially stepping down. The reception desk is mine.

It's not super interesting work, but it's straightforward enough (for the most part) and I get to see damn near the whole town at some point or another. It pays well enough and, most importantly, it allowed me to move back home.

By the time planting season comes around, I'm settled in nicely. I've gotten into the flow of things at work, reconnected with some high school friends, and am slowly starting to remember all the ways I used to belong here, instead of just the ways I didn't.

Spring turns into summer, and though our first harvest doesn't turn a huge profit, we've just barely in the black. Not bad for my first season after years away. Summer's profit is slightly higher, and by autumn it's looking like I really might be able to do this.

As we approach the anniversary of me moving back, I think a lot about my parents. There's a part of me that wishes I'd moved back before they died, but I think if I had, I would have pushed myself too hard to prove to them—and to myself—that I belonged here. Not that they ever made me feel like I had to prove it to them, but that's how disabilities work sometimes; they twist your thoughts until you're convinced you don't belong in the very spaces you need the most.

Besides, if I'd had my parents to support me when I moved back, I'm not sure the plow would have showed itself to me—it certainly never did in all the years they were alive, and it had ample opportunity to.

Anniversaries pass: Jensen and Cole's wedding; my parents' death; my return to the farm; the first time the plow and I fucked. They're a mix of bitter and sweet, but that's life, isn't it?

At the beginning of December, Jensen, Cole, and a couple of our friends are over at the house, when Jensen sits bolt upright from his spot on the floor in front of the couch. "Jackie!" he yells, as loud as he always gets when he's drunk. "Jackie! You should have a Christmas party."

Every single person in the room gives him a look. Of all of us, I'm the least likely to throw a party. The work involved would take too much out of me.

"No, no, no," he says, swaying toward me. His cheek lands on my knee, but he barely seems to notice. He just turns up to look at me with wide puppy-dog eyes. "Think about it." He stops, like *he* needs to think about it. Then he finally settles on "It would be fun."

And, well, I can't argue with him on that.

So we plan, and three weeks later, I throw a party. It's the kind of party I could have used a year ago, on my first Christmas back: a party for everyone who doesn't have family to spend it with. A party for everyone with nowhere to go—or who needs an excuse to leave their other celebrations a little early. We string up lights all across the closest field, since we don't have anything overwintering there, and haul out blankets, chairs, and the makeshift stage my dad used to use for parties.

The turnout is bigger than we expected, and I tear up at the sight of it. Last year's quiet celebration with Jensen, Cole, and their parents was lovely, but this is lively in a way the farm often used to be. There's almost a hundred people, and I'm sure more will show up as the night goes on.

I lose myself in the music, in the drinks, in this community I somehow managed to convince myself I could live without.

It's truly the perfect night, even if both my wrists and my back are braced because I pushed myself a little too hard setting up.

Around midnight, I notice a figure at the edge of the field, just barely visible in the darkness. I make excuses and pull myself away from my current conversation, then walk out into the night, going far enough to where I know nobody can see me.

I hear the telltale sound of blades in soil and metal lightly scraping metal, but I don't turn around until I've put almost a whole field's length between us and the party. You never know who else might have the same idea and sneak out into the night for a tryst of their own.

"I've missed you tonight," I breathe, stepping forward and pulling the plow into my arms. All those people at that party, and it's the plow I wanted most. The plow I thought about kissing when the alcohol started coursing through my veins.

If I'm being honest, I thought about a whole lot more than kissing.

I drop to my knees and suck one of the handles into my mouth. It tastes slightly earthy without the latex between us, but my lips stretch around it like it was made to slide between them, and I moan at the fullness against my tongue. I swirl my tongue around the wood, and the plow bucks, pushing itself deeper into my mouth. I suck until I can't take it anymore. I *need* it inside me, pounding away the pulsing ache between my legs.

I lie back and pull my dress up to my waist. I'm not wearing anything underneath.

The plow enters me in one swift move and I cry out, only hoping the sounds of the party a field away will swallow my cries. Even if someone hears, hopefully they'll assume it's a couple that sneaked away and not come over here to investigate.

A second later, any thought of being caught flies out of my mind as the plow thrusts again, hard and fast, the way it was scared to do that first time. It fucks me almost desperately, and I meet its every move with desperation of my own. I need it harder, faster, deeper, and I'm a whining, moaning mess within seconds. It doesn't let up, even when I clench around it and my orgasm rolls through me.

My first orgasm, I should say. Because it keeps fucking me and within minutes another one builds, higher and higher until it hits even harder than the first. I drench the ground with my come, soaking the ground in my essence.

The plow finally slows, fucking me sweet and slow as we ride out my orgasm together.

When it finally moves to pull out of my I grab it just below the handle to keep it firmly inside me. It feels so good, and I'm not ready for this moment to end. Not yet.

It's still for a few minutes, and when it slowly pumps in and out of me again, I jerk with every slide of the wood inside me. It's gentle, letting the gentle rolling of my hips set the pace, for which I'm grateful—there's not much more I can take, even though I'm not ready to stop fucking the plow.

My third orgasm is slower and deeper than the others, a building pressure and a gentle wave rather than the explosive crash of the first two. At the exact moment it crests, I swear I hear someone say "That's it, love. You look so beautiful when you come undone for me."

But it's all in my head. There's nobody here but me and the plow. And that's exactly how I want it to be.

ALSO BY ANNARA LAYNE

Sentient Object Romance
Objects of Desire

Bedding the Bedding

Plowing the Plow

Railing the Railing

* * *

Other Works
Obscure Holidays Erotica Collection (short stories)

Polar Bear Plunge

Clean off your Desk Day

Ditch New Year's Resolution Day

Hot Sauce Day

Eat Ice Cream for Breakfast Day

Work Naked Day

International Condom Day

Random Act of Kindness Day

Tell a Fairy Tale Day

Dentists Day

Napping Day

Awkward Moments Day

Make Up Your Own Holiday Day

ACKNOWLEDGMENTS

Plowing the Plow is the follow-up to Bedding the Bedding. While they're stand-alones, writing this gave me a glimpse into the difficulties of writing a sequel. I am so grateful for the many people who have supported me through this process.

As always, thanks to the bi+ book gang for the writing sprints that kept me going, and the cottage for all the support as I wrestled with book two in the Objects of Desire series (and, of course, thank y'all for brainstorming the series name with me). Thanks for holding my hand and cheering me on and coming along for the ride. I will always and forever appreciate y'all.

Many thanks to Bailey, for the blurbs. I don't know what I would have done without you.

When I picked up the first sentient object book I ever read, I went into it expecting silly fun—and it absolutely delivered on that front, but I wasn't expecting the amount of heart in it. I'm not claiming that my own books are super groundbreaking or anything, but many of the books I've read in this genre blend the funny and absurd with some really powerful emotional journeys, social commentary, and other elements that make them really resonate with a lot of people.

So for this series, that's what you can expect. Silly smut with a hefty dose of a character journey for the MC. Don't get me wrong, you can probably expect some stories from me in the future that are purely silly bullshit fun, because those stories absolutely have a place, and I've personally clung to those types of stories as a lifeline.

In the meantime, if this is your first sentient object romance (and even if it's not), I recommend looking into some of the other authors writing in this genre. Whether you're looking for silly fun, titillation, emotional journeys, or social commentary (or some blend of those), I can pretty much guarantee there's someone writing what you're looking for.